Susanna.

Sandy ran... ...ly and knelt down beside her ... ...o her feet. "Lassie! Are you all right?" The concern on his face struck her forcibly, and his strong arms helping her to her feet felt so warm and comfortable that she was reluctant to be released from them.

"Perhaps if I put my arms around your neck," she suggested, and he moved closer to comply with this request, placing his arms about her waist at the same time and thus managing to lift them both to a standing position.

Sandy was not a very tall man, but he was just the right height for Susannah, and her head fit comfortably against his shoulder once they were upright.

The temptation was too great, and Sandy was only a man, after all, not a stick of wood who could not be moved by such close proximity to a lady as beautiful as Susannah. He drew her closer and kissed her and in the heat of the moment did not notice that she was planted firmly on two feet to meet his embrace.

Other Fawcett Titles
by Denice Greenlea:

A FRIEND OF THE FAMILY
DISTANT RELATIONS

BIRCHWOOD HALL

Denice Greenlea

FAWCETT CREST • NEW YORK

A Fawcett Crest Book
Published by Ballantine Books

Copyright © 1984 by Denice Pipkin

All rights reserved under International and Pan-American Copyright
Conventions. Published in the United States by Ballantine Books, a
division of Random House, Inc., New York, and simultaneously in
Canada by Random House of Canada Limited, Toronto.

Library of Congress Catalog Card Number: 84-90878

ISBN 0-449-20122-8

All the characters in this book are fictitious and any resemblance to
persons living or dead is purely coincidental.

Manufactured in the United States of America

First Ballantine Books Edition: July 1984

❧ CHAPTER ONE ❧

Traveling through Duxtonbury, a passenger on the mail coach could not be faulted for thinking it a sleepy, rustic place where nothing ever happened. The single inn was not even large enough to be considered as a refreshment stop for the coach on its journey north from London, and when the coach did pause momentarily to deliver a few letters and half a dozen London newspapers, the passengers were not encouraged to alight. Instead, they remained secure in the coach to gaze out of the windows in a condescending manner and wonder when they would ever see civilization again.

The entire town could be viewed from the vantage point of one of the outside seats. The High Street was no longer than a few hundred yards, with no more than a dozen houses and shops on either side. Two dirt lanes ran off from it, one leading to the church, which occupied a

1

hilltop to the right overlooking the town, and one that branched off from the main road at the end of the town. Next to the church was a small cemetery and a large meadow, the only place in Duxtonbury where public gatherings could be held, for the village boasted no assembly hall, no theater, indeed no amenity of modern life the London traveler would consider essential to his well-being and happiness.

If the coach were early—a rare occurrence—a passenger might catch a glimpse of old Sam Larkin loafing about in the inn yard, waiting for a chum to come along and stand him a pint of bitter. More often, Sam was inside the taproom, already on his third pint by the time the coach arrived, and the only living soul to be seen was young Tim Travers, who collected the post from the coachman before hitching up his dog cart and delivering it to the correct parties.

Duxtonbury was only one of a hundred such villages the mail coach passed through on its journey north. As it gave such a lifeless and remote appearance, the urban-minded passenger might be tempted to think, conceitedly, that the arrival of this very coach in which he rode, bearing as it did messages and literature from the outside world, was the only event of any importance that took place there. In so thinking, he would be very much mistaken. Despite appearances, the village of Duxtonbury was swarming with life, and the residents therein gave as little regard to the daily appearance of the mail coach as they would to a stray cat. News from London was welcome, of course, but usually had no more importance for them than ancient legends or fairy stories. They had better things to think about and better ways of spreading information than by means of smudgy and ill-spelled sheets of lies delivered from London.

The news of Duxtonbury was spread by word-of-mouth, and lest any scorn this medium as simplistic or primitive, be assured that it was much speedier and at least as accurate as the greatest London newspaper. Indeed, if lines could be drawn on a map of the area, tracing the progress of a single item of news from one person to the next, they would describe an intricate network, with no farm, no lonely cottage or hut, so isolated or remote as to be left out of the pattern.

For example, on this very day, scarcely an hour after the mail coach had stopped and delivered its daily news from London, something of real import happened, in the shape of another coach that passed swiftly through the town and did not keep to the main road but took the fork to the right, which led to the ducal estate of Westham Park.

One of the first to notice this most interesting event was Mrs. Maggins, the local dressmaker, who was in the process of selling some darning cotton to Miss Lucy Grainly of Birchwood Hall. Her sharp eyes did not miss the ducal shield on the side of the carriage as it trundled by her window even as she handed Miss Grainly change from a crown.

"Now I'll be dipped in tar if that wasn't the duke of Duxton's coach just went by!" she exclaimed, not to Miss Grainly in particular, but to the world at large. "Whatever is the duke coming home for in the middle of the season? Very odd, I should say."

Her sighting was confirmed by Trunkett, Miss Grainly's maid. Although one of her eyes had a cast to it, no one had ever questioned the sharpness of its sight.

"It was not the duke himself inside, but Lord Westbridge,'' Trunkett declared, and as she was closer to the window and not carefully counting out shillings at the same time, the other two women were not disposed to doubt her.

"Lord Westbridge!" Miss Grainly exclaimed, and if Trunkett had not been so engrossed in watching the carriage to the very end of the High Street she would have noticed her mistress's sudden high color and reported it later to Lady Grainly as an "interesting thing." But by the time Trunkett turned away from the window, Lucy's face had regained its normal pale hue and she was carefully counting her change into her reticule.

"I agree with you, Mrs. Maggins," Trunkett said. "It is very odd indeed that any of the duke's family should return to the country in the middle of the season, especially his lordship."

"And with no warning, neither," Mrs. Maggins added with a nod of her head. "Little Sally Jeffers was in here but yesterday and with never a word about it, and she would know if anyone did, nor would she have been wasting her time buying ribbons for her hair if the family were expected, for I've heard her complain often enough how she's set to polish all the brass whenever they return."

"Sally Jeffers," Trunkett said, a gleam in her wandering eye as she pursued this tangent. "She must be all set to fasten onto Jem Tucker if she's decking herself out with ribbons now."

"I do believe they will be publishing the banns any day now," Mrs. Maggins told her with a knowing smile.

"Oh, how lovely," Lucy put in. "Jem is a tenant of ours."

The two older women nodded at her in recognition of her

superior social status and nothing more, for what she had said was not news but common knowledge.

A happy idea occurred to Mrs. Maggins and she eagerly tested it on Trunkett. "Perhaps that is why Lord Westbridge has returned so suddenlike. They do say he's been out seeking a wife in London this season." Who "they" were she did not need to make clear; this, too, was common knowledge.

"I'll wager you're right there, Mrs. Maggins," Trunkett answered. "They say he has sore need of a wife, since Lord Ingram married that heathen in the West Indies." She lowered her voice and glanced at her mistress to see if she was listening, but Lucy had wandered over to look at some French lace, a shilling a yard, remembering her mother's strictures against gossiping with servants.

"That story is true, then?" Mrs. Maggins asked in a hushed voice, knowing perfectly well that it was, but anxious to hear it confirmed once more. There was some news that did not grow stale in the retelling.

"Oh, yes, indeed," Trunkett assured her. "Mrs. Collins of Westham Park has told me that he already has four children by her, although whether they are properly married is anybody's guess!" Her voice had dropped to almost a whisper by now, to save her mistress's ears from such tales of debauchery.

"Well, Mrs. Collins should know if anyone does," Mrs. Maggins agreed. "She's been with the family since Lord Westbridge was a lad."

"Indeed, and she gets her news straight from Lady Imogen herself, who is the only one of her family who continues to correspond with her brother." She shook her head knowingly. "It would be disastrous should Lord Westbridge fail to beget an heir, and allow the dukedom to descend on Lord Ingram's family. They even say if he returned to England he would be hanged straightaway as a traitor. Not a pretty picture, eh, Mrs. Maggins?''

Mrs. Maggins clicked her tongue expressively. ''It seems such a shame. Lord Ingram was always such a merry little chap, not at all like his elder brother, who is such a sobersides. Still,'' she said cheerfully, reverting to her normal tone of voice, ''if Lord Westbridge has returned now it must mean he has been successful in London.''

''A wedding at Westham Park!'' Trunkett exclaimed. ''Now, won't that be a fine thing, eh, Miss Lucy? There hasn't been a wedding there since the duke married the first duchess, and I was but a girl then and you weren't even born.''

''Yes, it would be very fine,'' Lucy agreed unenthusiastically. ''Come, Trunkett, it is time we were getting home. Mamma will fret if we are too long.''

''And how is your poor mother, Miss Lucy?'' Mrs. Maggins asked solicitously.

''She suffers much from the pain in her hands,'' Lucy told her, ''but she does not like the drops the doctor has prescribed for her, as they make her heart flutter.''

''The poor, suffering woman. Has she tried a copper bracelet, then? Me granddam used to suffer terribly from the arther-itis until she got herself a pair of copper bracelets.''

''I will suggest it to her, Mrs. Maggins.''

''And mind you, tell her I was askin' after her, too, Miss Lucy, and that if she was wishful of obtaining a pair of them bracelets I know just the place to get them.''

''I will tell her that, Mrs. Maggins,'' Lucy said pleasantly. ''Good day to you.''

Mrs. Maggins shook her head sadly as she watched the young lady exit with Trunkett trailing faithfully behind. It was a shame that such a sweet girl with such a kind nature had never married. She probably never would be married now, for whatever prettiness she had possessed as a child had fled with the passing of the years. Mrs. Maggins was warmhearted enough to shed a brief tear over such a waste.

Then she brightened, remembering that she had news to impart, and went eagerly to the back room, where her dressmaking business was carried out, ready to spread the word of Lord Westbridge's return and imminent marriage to the two village girls who sewed for her.

However, Mrs. Maggins was premature in her anticipation of nuptial delights at Westham Park. While the news network of Duxtonbury managed to encompass the entire countryside, it occasionally developed a snag or two that needed to be put right. Mrs. Maggins would be put right later, when she took tea with her dear friend Mrs. Stark, who heard the full and correct story from Tim Travers when he delivered her post, who had it from Will Tucker, whom he met on his route, who had it from his elder brother, Jem, who had it straight from the kitchen at Westham Park.

With lightning speed all the servants at Westham Park were made aware of the circumstances behind the young master's return, as was Jem Tucker, who was calling upon Sally Jeffers. Sally was set to polish the brass as soon as she had heard her fill, and Jem set off for home. As he went he spread the tale to Lucas Johnson, Sam Arnold, and Miss Susannah Grainly, niece to Miss Lucy, who was out riding on her pony.

Miss Grainly lost no time in carrying the news to others on the Birchwood estate, including the Crocketts and the

Winnows. Mary Winnow was hanging out her washing, but Susannah did not consider it beneath her dignity to help with this task and, taking up the basket of pegs, proceeded to hand them out, one by one, as she brought Goodwife Winnow up-to-date on current events.

"Now, isn't that a shame," Mary said, shaking her head. "His father must be sore at heart to hear tell of such goings on."

"Indeed, I doubt that he has heard of it," Susannah said, "for his lordship came here straight from the scene of his disgrace, and the duke is still in town." She handed out a peg.

"There, that's the last of it," Mary said, fastening the peg and taking the basket from Susannah. "I thank you kindly for your help, Miss Sukey." She received a warm smile in reply and thought again, as she had of late, that Miss Sukey was turning into a real beauty. She was no more than a little bit of a thing in a shabby old riding habit, but her form was lithe and graceful, her fair hair hung in ringlets down her back, and her large brown eyes were fringed by unexpectedly dark lashes. A light sprinkling of freckles powdered her nose, but so far from detracting from the delicate lines of her features, they gave an impression of health and a life spent much out-of-doors. Aye, Mary sighed to herself, a real beauty, and though she appeared to be no more than thirteen, Mary's memory was long and accurate, and she wondered what Sir Basil was about to let his daughter run wild as though she were no more than a child.

"Will you stop and have summat to bite with me?" Mary invited cordially.

"No, thank you, Mary. I must be getting on home soon and I want to stop at the Lewis farm first."

All of Mary's misgivings rose to the surface. "Now, miss, it's not my place to say, but I can't help noticin' you've been spendin' a mighty amount of time visitin' with that foreigner, MacDougal." To her provincial mind, anyone born more than twenty miles outside of Duxtonbury was a foreigner. "Never you forget that he's a bachelor all alone there, and who knows what he was before. He never speaks of himself, that one."

Susannah laughed off this warning. "Now, Mary, you must not misjudge Sandy simply because he is a newcomer. He is quite as industrious as any of the farmers at Birchwood."

"It's not that what worrits me, miss. He's a hard worker, right enough, and always willin' to lend a hand. He helped Robin put in that new fence and has cleared away near thirty acres of the Lewis farm."

"There, you see how you are set against him? Old Lewis has been dead for two years now. How long must Sandy live there before we all start calling it the MacDougal farm?"

"Long enough, I reckon," Mary said. "You just mind yourself well, miss, when you're visitin' him. He's not like the rest of us, you know."

"I will take care, Mary, never you fear." Susannah laughed, mounting her pony and trotting off to the Lewis farm with a light heart.

Since Sandy MacDougal's arrival at Birchwood, she always saved this stop for last so she could spend as much time as possible with the newest tenant, for indeed, as Mary had said, he was not like the rest of them. With the others, Susannah was always mindful of her station as Sir Basil Grainly's daughter. While she might gossip with the Tuckers or the Winnows, they never forgot who she was, but always deferred to her respectfully. She could never claim true friendship with any one of them, but Sandy was different. He was not disrespectful, but neither did he grovel before her. Since their first meeting, when he had spoken in a Scottish burr so thick she could scarcely understand him, his attitude had been more that of a fond elder brother than a tenant farmer. She had grown accustomed to his accent, or else it had been softened by exposure to the gentler voices he heard around him, and had discovered in him a friend, someone she could talk to on her own level, who understood her jokes, who sympathized with her woes.

Indeed, to Susannah all the things that made the other farmers wary of him made him more interesting in her eyes, especially his mysterious past. By now she was quite convinced that he was escaping an unhappy love affair; some Scottish lassie had rejected his suit because he was no more than a penniless farmer, so he had forsaken the land of his forefathers and Bonnie Prince Charlie to eke out a lonely existence in the English countryside, where nothing familiar would remind him of his lost love.

Susannah found him working on his kitchen garden today, which was laid out next to his little thatched cottage. She never had any trouble spotting him wherever he might be working, on account of his red hair, a feature Susannah had never found attractive in a man until now. He was a handsome man otherwise, about eight-and-twenty years of age, not tall of stature, but broad-shouldered and muscular. His features were regular and pleasing, and his clear blue eyes always seemed to have laughter lurking in their depths.

"Ho! Sandy!" she called out as she rode up to the gate, full of her news.

Upon hearing her hail he straightened up, quickly tucked

away a book he had been consulting, and wiped the dirt from his trousers. Susannah never remarked upon his preoccupation with this volume, although she had seen him often with it. She supposed—no, she was certain—it was a collection of poetry he and his lost love had shared together. As he always hid it away when she came, obviously any reference to it would be painful for him.

"I have the loveliest bit of news to share with you," she said cheerfully as she dismounted and tethered her pony to a rail. "It concerns Lord Westbridge."

"Lord Westbridge?" he asked.

"The duke of Duxton's son and heir—I have told you all about him," Susannah explained patiently.

"Forgive me, child, I havena been studyin' my catechism as I ought," he said with a grin. "Lord *Westbridge*, of course! And what is this wee bit o' news you have to tell?"

"He has returned today," she announced.

"Weel, now, that's fine," he said, beaming. He was trying very hard, with Susannah's aid, to become part of the community, and supposed that if the community at large would react with pleasure at hearing of Lord Westbridge's return, why, then so should he.

"Are those peas you have planted there?" she asked, looking at where he had been working.

"Aye," he said, following her glance.

"Oh dear, they're not doing very well, are they?" Susannah said with a little giggle. "And your carrots want thinning, don't they?" Then seeing a slight look of distress on his face, she added soothingly, "But never mind. You could not have planted them any earlier, after all. You had two years' worth of weeds to clear away first."

"Aye, that's true enough," he agreed, remembered ruefully the aching shoulders that task had afforded him. "Come and bide wi' me here, lassie. Surely you have more to tell o' this Lord Westbridge." He led her over to the doorstep, where they could sit in the shade, and pulled out his pipe and tobacco pouch.

"Indeed I do, Sandy. It is the most amazing news I have heard in months."

"Then out wi' it, lassie, before you burst." He filled his pipe and proceeded to light it.

"Do you remember how I told you that Lord Westbridge has been looking for a wife lately?" she began.

"Now that you mention it, I do indeed. Somethin' about his younger brother marryin' a heathen in foreign parts, so he must marry himself to get an heir."

"That's right," Susannah said, pleased that he had remembered. "But Sandy, whatever you do, do not ask Lord Westbridge himself about his brother if you should chance to meet him—Lord Ingram is never mentioned."

"I wouldna be doin' that in any case," Sandy assured her. "Nor am I likely to meet this Lord Westbridge in the natural way o' things, nor know him if I passed him in the fields or such."

"Oh, you would know him well enough," Susannah giggled, "for he has returned to Westham Park with a broken nose and two black eyes!"

"Aye, that would mark a man," Sandy agreed soberly.

This subdued reaction did not satisfy Susannah, and she gave a great sigh and said, disappointed, "I suppose not knowing him, you cannot appreciate how truly amusing it is. Lord Westbridge has always been so dignified, so *proper*, that it is quite incredible he should have been bested in a bout of fisticuffs. One could more easily picture him with pistols at dawn, or in a sword fight . . .

but *fisticuffs*—'' she finished her sentence with an expressive shrug of her shoulders.

"It must have been somethin' important to drive the man to such a pass," Sandy suggested.

"Yes, indeed!" Susannah explained eagerly. "According to Robert Coachman, he found himself a bride in London, just as he was supposed to, but she was already betrothed to someone else. So he tried to steal her away and bring her to Westham Park—he *said* to marry her, but if someone is wicked enough to steal another man's fiancée, who knows what other wickedness he might be capable of?"

"Indeed," Sandy agreed, enjoying her tale even as he wondered how much was true and how much Susannah might be adding for dramatic effect.

"Of course, he did not succeed in his evil purpose, for the lady's fiancé came after them and challenged Westbridge and they had a great fight in the center of the town that all the countryside turned out to see, and Westbridge lost the fight and the lady. Now he has returned home to recover from his wounds before he goes back to London to find another wife." She sighed wistfully. "Oh, I *do* wish he could have made it all the way back to Duxtonbury with her, for then we could have seen the fight ourselves."

"Now, that's naught a young lassie like yourself would want to see," Sandy told her.

"Yes, I should," she disagreed. "Especially with Lord Westbridge as one of the contenders. He is such a pompous fool, I would dearly love to see him brought down a notch. I wonder what the lady looked like," she continued reflectively. "She must have been beautiful indeed to have two gentlemen fighting over her."

"Not so handsome if she ran off with another man," Sandy pointed out, sucking on his pipe.

13

"But she didn't run off with him!" Susannah protested. "Westbridge *stole* her." She sighed again. "It must be lovely to be stolen—but not by Westbridge, of course."

Sandy laughed. "I shouldna think it would be a comfortable thing to be stolen at all. There you are, goin' about your daily business, no trouble to anyone, and whoosh— next minute you're grabbed up and stuffed into a carriage and taken away to some place you dinna want to be. Very uncomfortable, I should think."

"I suppose you are right, Sandy," she agreed reluctantly. "But I expect I shall never know for certain. I will probably end up like poor Aunt Lucy, on the shelf, catering to grandmamma's every whim."

"Now, now," he said, patting her hand companionably. "You're too young yet to be worryin' about bein' on the shelf, lassie."

"Yes, I suppose I am," she agreed without meeting his eye. She knew very well that if Sandy was aware of her true age, he would not be sitting here so close to her, his hand gently resting on hers, a circumstance she found to be quite pleasant indeed. No, he would jump away from her in horror and pull on his forelock and call her "miss" instead of "lassie" or "child," and their beautiful friendship would be over forever. A child of the manor might make friends with whomever she chose, but once she became a young lady she must learn her place and keep to it. Susannah would make no such startling revelations today, nor any other day if she could help it.

They sat in comfortable silence for a few minutes, Sandy sucking on his pipe, Susannah enjoying the pungent smell of his tobacco. For the moment they did not need to speak; each was content with the other's company.

Presently, Susannah stretched her arms and remarked

lazily, "I suppose I should be getting back to the Hall. Grandmamma frets so when I am late for tea."

"And I should be gettin' back to my poor abused peas and carrots," Sandy said.

He walked back with her to her waiting pony and helped her up.

"I shall see you again tomorrow, Sandy," she promised.

"Aye, I'll be lookin' forward to that—providin' you havena been stolen away by then."

She laughed and wished him good day, and he watched her trot away, her slender figure straight and sure on the back of her little pony, her golden hair hanging loose down her back.

Unknowingly, he echoed Mary Winnow as he thought to himself, Aye, she'll be a beauty when she's grown a bit, and I hope I'll be here to see it.

❧ CHAPTER TWO ❧

THE NEWS OF Lord Westbridge's fall from grace and return to Westham Park was late in reaching Birchwood Hall. Lucy and Trunkett returned from their shopping expedition full of false suppositions, and there was no one there to put them right. Trunkett went into the kitchen, to share the news with Cook, and Cook told her husband, Simons. These three retainers comprised the entire staff of the Hall, there was not even a stable boy employed there who could rush in and beg a piece of cake from Cook in return for the true tale from Robert Coachman.

It had not always been thus at the Hall. Once, the graceful mansion had been full of chambermaids and parlormaids and pages and grooms. Once, the elegant chambers, which now stood silent and shrouded, had sparkled with finery. The now shabby draperies had been lustrous; the now threadbare carpets had softened the footsteps of the richly dressed residents. Silver and crystal had glittered on the dining table, where meals of twenty courses were once served, with a different wine for each course. Roaring fires had warmed the rooms in the winter, and in the summer there was always a servant about who would bring a refreshing drink, perhaps serving it in the formal garden, which was now choked with weeds.

That was how things had been when the seventh baronet, Sir Roland Grainly, had come into his inheritance. He was a handsome, cheerful man, well loved by his tenants and sought after by every marriageable young lady in the county. He chose as his bride Miss Agatha Winslow, who had little beauty and no fortune, but an abiding affection for her new husband. This affection was sorely tested during the years of her marriage, for while Sir Roland had but a single vice, it was a grave one. He could not resist any game of chance, and because he was a gentleman he considered it beneath his dignity to play for any but the highest stakes. The Grainly fortune had been large enough to support this drain of capital for many years, but eventually even the deepest well must run dry, and Sir Roland's fortune dwindled away until there was nothing left but the house itself and the lands it stood on, and these were entailed.

Sir Roland returned to Birchwood a broken man. He proceeded to drink himself into an early grave, leaving behind a depleted estate, a young son whose school fees must be found somewhere, and a baby daughter—the last relic of the affection Lady Grainly had once felt for him.

Sir Basil Grainly held only the vaguest recollections of Birchwood Hall as it once had been. He took over the reins of the estate from his mother when he attained his majority and had been scraping and scrabbling ever since.

Lady Grainly, fearing that he might exhibit the same wicked tendencies as his father, exerted perhaps too great an influence over him. The one and only time Sir Basil had ever gone against his mother's wishes was in the matter of his marriage. Lady Grainly had chosen Lady Imogen Westham as his bride—she was handsome and wealthy, and an alliance with the Westham family would have done much to restore the fortunes of the Grainlys. However, Sir Basil was some years older than Lady Imogen and impatient to marry. He chose as his bride Miss Frances Wigget, the vicar's daughter, and Lady Grainly had never forgiven him for this single act of disobedience. Fanny did not even produce an heir for Birchwood. Her sole progeny was Susannah, and upon producing this tiny replica of herself, she went into a decline that lasted ten years before her death. Nor did she win Lady Grainly's approval by finally removing herself from Birchwood. Lady Imogen, who was now quite old enough to be married, had already married another.

Lady Grainly then pinned her hopes of a Westham alliance on her daughter, Lucy. Lucy had grown up with the Westham children and had both Lord Westbridge and Lord Ingram to choose between, but nothing ever developed in that quarter. Lady Grainly had given up the struggle in disgust.

Lucy was well aware of the disappointment she had been to her mother. Today, with Lord Westbridge's return, she had been most sharply reminded of it. She entered the drawing room, the only downstairs room besides the dining room that was left unshrouded for general use, fully expecting the reproachful comments she would receive when she told her mother of Lord Westbridge's approaching marriage. Lady Grainly was not in the drawing room, however, and so Lucy was afforded an unusual privacy for her own reflections. She sat behind the harpsichord and plucked out a little air, but the instrument was so far out of tune that the sound it produced was discordant and unpleasing to her ear. So she took a seat beside her workbox and proceeded to mend stockings with the darning cotton she had recently purchased.

Presently, a single tear trickled down her cheek, and she dashed it away impatiently. She had had long years to grow used to the idea that Lord Westbridge would marry some day; it was silly and fruitless to cry over it now. She sighed and gazed out the window, recalling a time some twelve years before when her hopes that he might chose *her* as his bride had not seemed so foolish. That lovely summer had been the happiest time of her life. Lord Westbridge, Ivor, as he was to her then, had finished his degree at university and was preparing to take his commission. Oh, the arguments they had had on that subject! As the eldest son he had no reason or need to take a commission and risk his life on the battlefield, but he had insisted that honor demanded he defend his country in time of war, and no amount of pleading on her part could dissuade him from his purpose.

They parted with the coming of autumn; no promises had been exchanged between them, as Ivor did not know when or if he would return. On his last night they had strolled down to the Westham summer house and there exchanged a single kiss, the first for both of them. Had Lucy known then that that kiss must suffice her for the rest of her life, she might have asked for more, but in the fullness of her youth the future seemed as promising as Ivor's strong embrace.

In the years that followed they grew apart, and Lucy had

neither the wiles nor the spirit to pursue him as so many others did. She simply reconciled herself to her spinsterhood and made a vow that she would welcome as a sister any bride Ivor brought home.

Lucy shook herself out of her reverie and applied herself to the task at hand. It would not do for her mother to find her sitting idle, daydreaming the afternoon away.

The news that was even now speeding its way into the farthest corner of the county had not yet reached the two senior members of Birchwood Hall, for they had been closeted together in the estate office for the last hour. This was not an unusual circumstance, as the precarious financial situation of the estate required frequent conferences between the keeper of the house and the keeper of the land. However, this conference had rather a different subject than the usual under discussion. It was a matter that had received Lady Grainly's neglect for too long, until this morning when she had heard an interesting thing from Trunkett. After pondering the problem all morning, Lady Grainly had come up with an adequate solution and was now ready to make her wishes known to her son.

"Basil, I must speak to you about your daughter," Lady Grainly announced, throwing open the office door in a dramatic manner and knocking the estate map from its precarious hold on the wall in the process. This she ignored.

Long years of his mother's sneaking up on him in just this way had told their tale on Sir Basil's nerves. He started violently in his chair, and the nervous tic on the right side of his mouth twitched. Not a tall man, he had been worn thin by his cares and seemed to shrink even more in his mother's presence. He also had a nervous habit of running his hand through his thinning hair, a habit—his mother had often warned him—that would only hasten his inevitable baldness.

"Sit down, mamma," he invited her, rising hastily to remove some books from the only other seat available besides his own. He returned to his place behind the desk, closing the ledger that he had been consulting, a volume remarkable mainly for its colorfully inscribed entries.

Lady Grainly set her ponderous form in the chair provided. Her gnarled fingers closed on the silver head of her walking stick. This and a gold eyeglass that hung about her neck were two items she was never without.

"What has Susannah done now?" Sir Basil asked wearily, trying to disguise the irritation in his voice. Working on his accounts always made him cross, especially when there was a chance his mother might wish to look them over, just as she had looked over his lessons when he was a small boy.

"It has come to my attention that she has been consorting with the tenants again," Lady Grainly announced in dire tones.

Sir Basil had heard this complaint before. "And where is the harm in that?" he asked, gallantly defending his daughter, who reminded him so pleasurably of his cherished Fanny. "There is no one else in the neighborhood for her to consort with, as you put it, now that the Middleton girls have both married and gone away."

"She can spend her days with Lucy and me, pursuing more suitable domestic occupations," Lady Grainly declared. "Has it escaped your notice, Basil, that Susannah is no longer a child? It is no longer appropriate for her to ride unaccompanied all over the estate, speaking to every young farmer she meets. Who knows what harm she may come to? Especially at the hands of a foreigner."

Sir Basil now recognized that the current focus of his mother's disapproval was the newcomer, Sandy MacDougal. From the first she had opposed the idea of a Scotsman tilling the soil of Birchwood; she had a deep and abiding prejudice against the Scottish.

"I doubt she would come to any *harm*," he said, "but I certainly agree that she should not be visiting him. It won't do—won't do at all. I shall speak to her on the subject."

"Of course you will. And remember this—if I hear that she continues her visits to the Lewis farm, I will hold *you* responsible, Basil." She put a hand briefly to her breast, as if to still the palpitations she was subject to were she crossed in any way. Sir Basil never had any cause to doubt the reality of these fluctuations of her vital organ. The outward signs of her other complaint, arthritis, were visible to the most casual observer in the swollen joints of her fingers and the stiffness of her gait. That one could not actually see a heart flutter was no reason to suppose that it did not, in point of fact, do so.

"However," Lady Grainly continued, her heart apparently calm once more, "I am afraid that a simple lecture will not suffice this time. We must strike at the root of the problem—we must consider Susannah's future. Are you aware, Basil, that your daughter will be eighteen in two months' time?"

Sir Basil, who always thought of Susannah as no more than twelve years of age at most, was surprised. "Eighteen?" he repeated, then as if to explain his lapse of memory, "She doesn't look it."

"Nor does she act it," Lady Grainly said grimly. "When I was her age I was already mistress of this house and expecting my first child. It is my considered opinion that the time has come for us to find a husband for Susannah."

Sir Basil had valiantly accepted the addition of six years to his daughter's supposed age, but the idea of marrying off his baby girl was almost too much for him. "Married?" he repeated incredulously, his mouth twitching. "But surely she is still too young to think of that yet."

"Need I repeat, Basil, that I was married at sixteen?"

"At sixteen? That is certainly too young. What was your father about to let you enter into matrimony at such a tender age?"

Lady Grainly thumped her cane against the floor with impatience. "You are straying from the point, Basil. It is not *my* marriage that is at question here. That, thankfully, is a completed chapter of my life and one I do not care to dwell on at any length."

Sir Basil did not contradict his mother, although he might have pointed out that she often dwelt upon that chapter, at great length. Instead, he merely said, "Yes, mamma."

"If you pause for reflection, you will see that I am right." The "as usual" was unspoken, but understood. "I will admit that I have been at fault in letting the girl run wild. For that I will answer to no one but God Himself on Judgment Day; to others I can only offer the excuses of my burdensome duties and failing health, which have left me little time to see to the finishing of her education. I propose to make amends on that score and prepare the girl for marriage as soon as may be."

"Yes, mamma," Sir Basil said. His little Sukey married— well, he supposed he would get used to the idea. "But whom is she to marry, mamma? There is no one in our acquaintance who would be suitable."

"That is a difficulty," she allowed, "but one that can be overcome if we set our minds to it. The obvious

23

solution is to enlarge our acquaintance. I have been think-ing long and hard about this, Basil, and I am well aware that some sacrifice must be made. The good Lord knows *that* should be no obstacle to me; my life has been an unending sequence of sacrifices. What, indeed, is one more?''

This was a familiar complaint of hers and one that by overuse failed to generate the proper amount of sympathy in her son's heart.

''What sacrifice were you thinking of this time, mamma?'' he asked, wondering what, indeed, was left to be sold. The last great sacrifice had been the plate, which had gone years before to help pay for the new roof; even the por-traits of the Elizabethan ancestors—a smaller sacrifice, but a sacrifice nonetheless—had been sold some time ago to a collector from London. All that was left of the once fine furnishings of Birchwood Hall was either shabby or in need of repair. The family jewels, like the estate, were entailed and could not be sold.

''There is only one thing I have left to me that is of any value,'' Lady Grainly said, bowing her head under the weight of her martyrdom. ''The only thing of value your father left to me. I had thought to leave it to Lucy, but I believe it will serve a better purpose now to sell it at last and use the proceeds for Susannah's benefit. My only fear is that the duke is no longer interested in making the purchase.'' She lifted her head to make the dire pronounce-ment, ''We must sell the Fifty Acres.''

''Ah,'' Sir Basil said, fearing it would be worse. The Fifty Acres was the only unentailed parcel of land on the estate. It was not farming land, but it was full of grouse and partridge and had once belonged to the Westhams, in times long past. An ancestral Grainly had married Lady

Winifred Westham, and this parcel was joined to Birchwood as part of her dowry. The present duke of Duxton, discovering some old maps of his estate in a long forgotten cubbyhole in his library, had come to Sir Basil with a generous offer to buy back the land, for he knew well that the money would be welcome. Sir Basil would have been more than willing to sell it immediately, but it was not his to sell. It had been left to Lady Grainly in Sir Roland's will, and she wouldn't hear of parting with it at the time. Indeed, the suggestion had caused her so much agitation that Sir Basil had feared for her life.

"Yes," Lady Grainly repeated, "we must sell the Fifty Acres."

"Why, I think that is a splendid idea, mamma," Sir Basil said with enthusiasm. "I am certain Duxton would be more than willing to buy it; he has often repeated his offer to me. But would it not be rather hard on Lucy? After all, you were planning to leave it to her; it should be used for her benefit." He brightened as an alternative occurred to him. "Why don't you find Lucy a nice, rich husband, and then *he* can help Susannah." He was quite pleased with himself for coming up with this, for he was fond of his little sister and would like to see her well placed.

Lady Grainly sighed. "I have long given up hope of Lucy's ever finding a husband, of whatever means. It cannot have escaped your notice, Basil, but Lucy is plain." It cost her much to make this admission, for Lucy was the very image of her mother in feature, if not in disposition. "And besides that, whatever chance she once might have had for making a match has certainly passed her by. She is two-and-thirty years of age."

"No!" Sir Basil protested. He had stopped reckoning his

sister's birthdays some ten years before, and to his mind she looked no older than the two-and-twenty he thought her to be.

"Susannah, however, shows some promise," Lady Grainly continued. "At least she resembles her mother, who was thought to be a beauty, although *I* could never see it. With the proper training, which I propose to give her, and a small amount of capital, she should be quite presentable in polite society. It is my intention to give her a season—not in London, of course, for we could never afford that, but friends of mine assure me that Bath is quite fashionable nowadays and not at all expensive. I believe I can have Susannah well enough in hand by next spring to present her in Bath with the reasonable expectation that there she will find herself a suitable husband."

"But I thought you detested Bath, mamma."

"It is true that I did not care for it when I went there to take the cure. Drinking the waters did nothing for my arthritis, and I refused to bathe in them. Indeed, the entire city was full of invalids, and the Assembly Balls were always a crush. However, correspondents of mine have assured me that the city has improved much in the twenty years since I visited it, and if it is still full of old men, then perhaps that might be just what Susannah needs to calm her wild nature. A rich widower would make an ideal husband for her, don't you agree, Basil?"

"Yes, mamma," he replied, not agreeing in the least.

"Then that is quite settled," Lady Grainly said, satisfied. "I think it best, however, to mention none of this to Susannah until the sale of the Fifty Acres is assured. You will write to the duke immediately."

"Certainly, mamma."

"In the meantime, you must speak to her about that

other matter, Basil. Make it clear to her that she is too old now to go gallivanting off wherever she pleases, especially if it is to call on unattached bachelors. In future, she will submit herself thoroughly to my direction.''

"Of course, mamma.'' Her mention of unattached bachelors had brought another idea to his mind, and his mouth twitched nervously as he wondered if he dared express it. Her next words made him bolder.

"You realize, Basil, that this is our last chance to find a fortune,'' she said, leaning on her walking stick and rising stiffly. "If my plans go awry we will have no further resources upon which to draw and must resign ourselves to living out our lives in poverty.''

"There *is* one other resource, mamma,'' Sir Basil suggested tentatively.

"What is that?'' she asked.

"I am sure you are aware of it; indeed, I have mentioned it to you before.'' His mouth twitched, and he ran his hand through his hair.

"Well?'' She now had some inkling of what was to come and fixed her son with an awful gaze.

Sir Basil licked his lips and whispered, "The heir— Alexander Grainly.''

Lady Grainly's fingers clenched convulsively over the head of her walking stick, and for a fearful moment Sir Basil thought she would strike him with it.

"Let me never hear you utter that name again! The Grainlys of Birchwood Hall will never accept charity, especially from one who has made his fortune in trade.''

"But mamma, it would not be charity,'' he said. "He would regard it as an investment in his inheritance. He certainly would not miss a few thousand pounds—since the end of the war the wine import business has been booming. He's quite a wealthy man—''

''Basil,'' Lady Grainly said, clutching at her breast as if she could manually still the wild beatings of her heart. ''I will try to forget you ever said that. I will only repeat what I have told you before. That man's money will never be used for the benefit of Birchwood Hall as long as I have breath in my body.''

''Don't you mean as long as *I* have breath in *my* body?'' Sir Basil suggested. ''After all, it is upon my death that he will inherit, and you may live many years after that.''

''This is not a time for levity, Basil. I have little doubt that I shall predecease you, especially if you insist upon bringing up the name of that—that *usurper*.''

''He is hardly a usurper, mamma—more like the heir apparent.''

''Heir presumptive, you mean,'' Lady Grainly corrected him, ''although I have given up all hopes of your remarrying. You have never done anything else to please me, why should I expect that?''

''That's rather hard, mamma,'' Sir Basil protested, arising. ''You know how I have always striven to please you, in all things.'' His mother seemed to be recovering her composure now, so he pressed on quickly. ''Now you know, mamma, that a few thousand pounds would fix us up nicely and you needn't think of it as charity. Alexander would be more than willing to give us a loan, with easy interest rates, on the strength of the family connection.'' He paced back and forth as he spoke, running his hand through his hair. ''Indeed, he was the one to approach me on the matter, for he has developed a keen interest in the estate, knowing that it will be his one day. And he has quite a head on his shoulders, mamma; he attended university in Edinburgh, took over the business upon his father's death, and increased profits one hundred percent in two years. In all my correspondence with him he has proven himself to be quite the gentleman, but then, after all, he *is* a Grainly.''

During this speech, two veins on his mother's neck had begun to throb and her face had turned an alarming shade of red. By the time she learned that he had actually been corresponding with the usurper, it seemed her head would burst from the pressure of suppressed rage, and burst it did, in the form of an agonizing, inhuman scream.

She sank back into the chair, and Sir Basil rushed to her side and attempted to revive her. Almost immediately, both Trunkett and Lucy burst in, for they could not have failed to hear that penetrating scream had they been seated in the drawing room of Westham Park. Trunkett uncorked the bottle of sal volatile she always had handy for just such an emergency.

''What has happened, Basil?'' Lucy asked in distress.

''I mentioned Alexander Grainly to her,'' he explained, stricken.

Lucy turned white. This dread name had been held up as a bogy to her for many years.

''Fetch some water, Miss Lucy,'' Trunkett commanded, and Lucy went to do as she was bid.

With the application of the salts and a few sips of the water Lucy quickly brought, Lady Grainly appeared to recover from her attack.

''Are you all right, mamma? Should we fetch the doctor?'' Lucy asked.

''No, no, I do not want the leech,'' she said crossly, and both her children sighed with relief, for this was a sure sign she was returning to herself.

"Would you like to lie down, mamma?" Lucy suggested.

"No, I would not. Lucy, help me to the drawing room. Trunkett, fetch the tea. I have need of refreshment." Lucy helped her up, but before she allowed herself to be led away, she turned to her son and said, "Basil, you will never speak to me on that subject again, unless you wish to be responsible for my death."

"Yes, mamma," Sir Basil replied miserably.

A few minutes later, after having partaken of some tea—the only luxury Lady Grainly afforded herself—she appeared to be quite herself once more. Her face had returned to its normal color, her breath was regular, and her heart was beating steadily in her breast.

"Mrs. Maggins was asking after you," Lucy ventured at last, when her mother appeared to be disposed once more for conversation.

"That is kind of her," Lady Grainly said, pouring herself another cup of tea.

"While I was in her shop, we saw the duke's carriage pass by, with Lord Westbridge inside." Her mother gave a small indication of interest, so Lucy continued. "Mrs. Maggins is quite convinced he has returned to announce his marriage."

At this reminder of her vain hopes for her daughter in that direction, she put her cup down with a clatter and said severely, "Lucy, how often have I told you not to gossip with your inferiors? It is ungraceful and unladylike. If Lord Westbridge is planning a wedding, then we will know it soon enough without listening to old women in shops."

"Yes, mamma," Lucy said mildly.

"It is especially unbecoming in you to speak of such a

thing as Lord Westbridge's marriage, for it can only remind me painfully of how you failed me in that regard.''

"Yes, mamma.''

"As you may have noticed, Susannah has already missed her tea, for she is no doubt committing the same fault at this very moment. Indeed, I have asked your brother to speak to her about it. I will depend upon you to set an example to her, Lucy.''

"Yes, mamma,'' Lucy said, and sighed.

❦ CHAPTER THREE ❧

THE TEA THINGS had been removed by the time Susannah made her breathless entrance. Her grandmother and aunt were busy with their correspondence and darning respectively, and the former did not even lift her head when Susannah made her announcement,

"You will never guess the latest tittle-tattle in the neighborhood!" she proclaimed with proper emphasis.

Her grandmother spared her one disapproving glance. "Susannah, you have missed your tea," she said shortly and returned to her task.

"If we shall never guess, perhaps you should tell us," Lucy suggested.

"Oh, no—you must at least try to guess. It is too comical!" She pushed her hair out of her face impatiently as she waited for a reply, but Lucy did not appear to be entering the game with the proper spirit. "Shall I give you a hint?" Susannah suggested.

"Susannah, how many times have I told you that riding apparel is unsuitable for the drawing room?" Lady Grainly inquired rhetorically. She lifted her eyeglass and through it examined the trail of Susannah's progress across the room. "You have tracked mud all over the carpeting. I hope you realize that you must clean it up yourself. Simons's back has been troubling him lately, and it is certainly neither Trunkett's nor Cook's place to clean the carpets."

"I will clean it up later," Susannah promised, her natural high spirits not the least whit stifled by her grandmother's daunting tones. "You simply *must* hear this first! Have you not guessed yet?"

Lucy gave her mother a helpless glance, then prompted, "You said you would give us a hint."

"Very well." She cleared her throat importantly. "*Who* do you suppose has returned to Westham Park?"

"Lord Westbridge, of course," Lady Grainly said. "We have heard all about it. It is common knowledge. Now will you have done with this absurd guessing game and go and change your clothes?"

Susannah's exuberance was somewhat deflated by this, as Lady Grainly had intended. "Then I suppose you have also heard why he has returned," she said, subdued but still hoping they had not.

Lady Grainly sighed. "It is said he has returned to announce his marriage and post the banns," she said, quite forgetting that she had chastised Lucy less than an hour ago for repeating this same piece of gossip. At the moment, she wished only to take the wind out of Susannah's sails long enough for the girl to remove herself and her muddy boots from the drawing room.

Instead, Susannah laughed gleefully and plopped herself unceremoniously into a chair. "There, I knew it! You have it all wrong! Would you care to hear the correct reason, which I have had straight from Robert Coachman, who was an eyewitness?"

Lady Grainly was annoyed. "How often have I told you not to listen to the gossip of servants?" she asked severely. Susannah supposed it was as often as she had been told about her riding apparel, but did not say so. "This instance simply proves the value of keeping that in mind," her grandmother continued. "Lucy came to me with a tale of his lordship's betrothal, which she learned from a *shopkeeper*, and now you wish to contradict it with a tale from a *coachman*. I suggest we wait to hear the news from Lord Westbridge himself. If he has anything of moment to impart, he will certainly call on us while he is in the neighborhood. Otherwise, it is apparent that the reason for his return is none of our concern."

Susannah giggled. "From what *I* have heard, he is in no condition to call upon anyone."

"Do you mean he is ill?" Lucy asked with sudden alarm.

"No, not exactly ill—but not in the first bloom of health, either," Susannah said, then added regretfully, "but as grandmamma has forbidden me to speak of it—" she shrugged her shoulders and rose from her seat.

"Sukey!" Lucy protested. "You *must* tell us now! Has he had an accident? If he is injured in any way we should know about it, in case he needs our help or care while he is at Westham Park. None of his family is there to look after him. Don't you agree, mamma?" she appealed.

Lady Grainly was weakening. Despite her best intentions, she was now bursting with curiosity herself. She nodded to

Susannah. "What Lucy says is quite true. We should know if Lord Westbridge needs our aid. I think, in this case, we can make an exception."

With this approval, Susannah lost no time in spilling out the whole story of Lord Westbridge's humiliation in a village square, a story that was for the most part true, except for certain dramatic embellishments Susannah saw fit to add.

"How dreadful!" Lucy said when the tale was ended, but her exclamation did not carry the full weight of conviction when she realized happily that Lord Westbridge was not to be married after all.

This circumstance did not escape Lady Grainly's notice either. A calculating look came over her face as she said with apparent indifference, "Perhaps I should invite him to dinner while he is in residence. Surely he would not mind coming amongst such old friends as we, however disfigured he may be. If he is all alone at Westham Park, he may be eager for company."

"Oh, I do hope he has not suffered any permanent disfigurement," Lucy said, distressed. "I have always found him so handsome."

"Yes, we know what you have always found, Lucy," her mother said unkindly, "and it is too bad you always lost it again. Go and change now, Susannah—and do not think that because I have listened to you this time I have changed my mind about your gossiping with servants. Indeed, your father will have a few words to say to you on that subject later."

"Yes, grandmamma," Susannah said obediently, satisfied now that she had shared her news and eager to go and do the same with Cook.

Lady Grainly and her daughter both appeared to return

to the tasks that had occupied them before Susannah's entrance, but Lady Grainly, for one, found it impossible to continue with the letter she had been writing. Even as she dipped her pen into the inkwell to sign her name with a flourish, it occurred to her that a trip to Bath would not be necessary at all now, thanks to Lord Westbridge's fickle fiancée. Apparently, his lordship was once again in need of a bride, and she was in an excellent position to provide one. The Fifty Acres would be worth far more as a dowry for Susannah than they would have been in an outright sale to the duke. Lady Grainly contemplated with pleasure how easily an alliance between the two families might be brought about to everyone's satisfaction. Putting down the pen with a sudden rap, she tore up the sheet she had been writing upon and rose stiffly to seek out her son for another interview about Susannah's future.

Lord Westbridge was not disposed to attend a dinner party, especially at the rustic and poverty-stricken Birchwood Hall, where they would no doubt serve leg of mutton from some ancient sheep, the very thought of which set his poor, abused jaw aching. He had groaned aloud when he read Lady Grainly's invitation and would have bestirred himself to write a refusal then and there, but when he lifted his aching head from his pillow to do so, the dizziness returned and he sank back again, calling out irritably, "Bissell! This cloth is not cold enough any more. Fetch me a fresh one!"

"Indeed, my lord," Bissell admonished, applying a fresh, cool cloth to his master's forehead, "it was not wise for you to have undertaken a journey in your present condition."

"Quiet, man, I cannot bear the sound of voices." Ivor

did not consider it necessary to explain to his valet that he could not have remained where he was—residing in the same inn as the man who had bested him and the woman who had jilted him. Nor could he yet return to London; it would be too humiliating. He had actually felt quite well that morning before he started out, and he had no doubt he would be well again by tomorrow morning. At least he was at Westham Park now, and he could remain here until his injuries healed and gossip had died down.

The invitation from Birchwood reminded him that there was just as much gossip in the country as in the city. No doubt the whole county knew by now that he had returned and why. The Grainlys must be eager to view the full extent of his reported injuries to have got an invitation out so quickly.

Then he remembered the part of the invitation mentioning that Sir Basil wished to speak to him on a matter of mutual benefit. Now, that was deuced queer. If Sir Basil wished to speak to one about a business matter, then why didn't the man simply call on one in the morning, like any civilized human being? Why drag one over to his shabby house to chew on tough mutton?

Ivor sighed and shifted the cloth on his head. If only this headache would go away he would be able to collect his thoughts and think clearly once more. He dreaded facing his father to tell him what had happened. Here he was, three-and-thirty years of age, heir to a dukedom and a considerable fortune, not ugly or deformed in any way, yet he had been unable to find a wife. Not only had he failed to find one, but he had botched his one concerted effort so spectacularly that it was unlikely any respectable female would even *speak* to him again once the story spread, let alone marry him. Not for the first time he cursed his younger brother for a traitorous scoundrel, for if Ingram had behaved himself and married a proper English wife, there would be no worries about the succession at all.

Where had he gone wrong? Ivor wondered. He had gone about the business so systematically, constructing a list of suitable brides to be judged on points of beauty, fortune, and intelligence. He had been so convinced that he had chosen correctly. Miss Durant earned high scores on all points and had even given every impression of being madly in love with him—a bonus. There was simply no telling, Ivor realized with regret. If only he could give up this whole business of looking for a bride; he had no heart for it now. If only someone would present him with a wife, neatly wrapped and tied and everything in order. He would accept her gladly, grateful that he would be spared suffering through another London season, shopping in the marriage mart.

His thoughts strayed back to the invitation from the Grainlys. If he refused, it would not stifle gossip, but only add to it; everyone would suppose that he was too ill to go out in company, and his injuries would be exaggerated accordingly. He wondered if he could bear an evening of boring conversation and tough mutton just to save his reputation and discover what Sir Basil wished to speak to him about that could possibly be of mutual benefit. It had better be important to warrant an evening spent with Lady Grainly. He recalled her with a shudder and remembered how she always seemed to regard him with disapproval when he was a child. He used to mimic her imperious, commanding tone for Lucy's amusement when they played together in the summer house, and while Ingram had always done a better imitation, Lucy had always laughed harder at his own.

Lucy, he thought sleepily. Lucy would be at dinner tomorrow night, and for some reason this knowledge warmed him. He remembered meeting her at the fête last summer and noticing how plain she had grown. She would end up looking just like her mother—no chin to speak of and pale eyes, but she still had the same sweet, quiet disposition she had as a child; fortunately, she would never resemble her mother in that respect. As a bride, Lucy would never meet any of his rigid standards, but as an old friend, she was more than satisfactory. He knew he could depend on her not to reproach him for his recent peccadillo, but to offer him sympathy and understanding. Lord knows, a fellow needed a dose of sincere admiration every once and a while to lift his spirits.

Very well, then, he would attend this deuced dinner party tomorrow, and if they served mutton he would cut it into very tiny pieces. He hoped fervently that they hadn't sold off all their sharp knives.

With this thought, he drifted off into fitful slumber.

At dinner that evening, Sir Basil Grainly seemed strangely preoccupied, and Lady Grainly dominated the conversation. They had received Lord Westbridge's acceptance of their invitation, and as she had much to occupy her mind in preparing for the dinner party, Lady Grainly had quite forgotten her attack of palpitations that afternoon. Lucy, of course, had told Susannah all about it while they were dressing for dinner, and her niece had turned quite as white as she had upon hearing the name of Alexander Grainly.

"What was papa about to mention him at all?" Susannah asked, amazed.

"I did not think it appropriate to inquire," Lucy told her, "and it is best you do not either."

"I should have no cause to do so," Susannah assured her. "Grandmamma already has enough fault to find with me. I should not care to give her further cause for reproof."

The name that *was* mentioned that night, and often, was that of Lord Westbridge. Lady Grainly discussed at length the preparations needed to entertain him in proper style.

"Lucy, you will have to mend the other tablecloth," she directed. "I noticed at least two new holes the last time we used it."

"Yes, mamma," Lucy said.

"Susannah, I will expect you to make certain the drawing room is in order, as you are the one who creates most of the disorder. Please remember to polish the fire irons, too. They are looking very dull lately."

"Yes, grandmamma," Susannah said.

Simons came in to remove the dishes and serve Sir Basil his small glass of port.

"Lucy, you will leave us," her mother commanded. "Your brother and I have something to discuss with Susannah."

"Yes, mamma," Lucy said, mystified but unquestioning.

"We have?" Sir Basil asked.

"Yes, we have," Lady Grainly assured him.

"Oh, yes! Of course we have!" He cleared his throat and assumed a deeper tone. "Susannah, we must ask you to curtail your visits to the tenants," he said.

"What do you mean?" Susannah asked, looking back and forth from her father to her grandmother. Their frowning faces were making her quite nervous.

"It is not proper for you to ride so far unaccompanied," Sir Basil continued, with a glance at his mother, who nodded.

"But I have always done so, papa. Besides, if I am

40

visiting with the tenants, then I am only unaccompanied for a short time, in between farms," she pointed out, hoping this would solve the problem.

"Exactly," her father said, "and that is why you need a chaperone—you should not visit the tenants alone."

Susannah was bewildered. "But who is to accompany me? Lucy does not care to ride, and there is no one else I can think of."

"Exactly," he repeated, "and that is why you must curtail your visits." He was pleased that he was making his points so quickly and precisely. "For example, I do not mind your visiting the Winnows or the Tuckers, but I must ask you to stay away from the Lewis farm. Sandy MacDougal is a bachelor, and it is most improper that you should spend time alone with him."

"But papa, Sandy is my friend!"

"Humph," Lady Grainly muttered. "Friend, indeed."

"It is most improper," Sir Basil said, gravely shaking his head. "I do not like to forbid you anything, my dear, but I am afraid I must put my foot down in this instance. You are to have nothing more to do with MacDougal."

"But papa!" Susannah cried, tears forming in her eyes. "Sandy is not like the other tenants. You would know better than I, but I believe he is a gentleman who has fallen into straightened circumstances."

"What utter nonsense!" Lady Grainly exclaimed, amazed by this fantasy.

"And I am quite sure he would never *harm* me," she continued, a catch in her voice.

"Nothing you can say will change my mind in this matter," Sir Basil said. "If I hear you have been visiting his cottage again, I will have to forbid you to ride altogether."

Lady Grainly was proud to see him take such a strong stand, and nodded her approval.

"But I don't understand. In what way could he harm me?"

Sir Basil ran his hand through his hair and looked to his mother to explain this delicate issue.

"A young lady always has one priceless possession," Lady Grainly began. "A spotless reputation. To keep that reputation spotless, she should refrain from visiting bachelors, especially bachelors of the lower orders, unaccompanied, for fear he might, er, *stain* that spotless reputation."

"But Sandy would never do anything like that," Susannah insisted. "First of all, he does not even know that I am a young lady—he thinks I am no more than a child. Besides that, I do not think he is of the lower orders at all, but a gentleman, as I have told you."

"Faugh," Lady Grainly said, disgusted. She nodded at her son to continue.

"There are no circumstances that will convince us to alter our decisions, Susannah," Sir Basil said firmly. "If MacDougal were a gentleman as you suspect—mind you, I am not saying he *is*, but *if* he were—then that would be even more reason to keep you from him. One day he would discover you are no longer a child, and if he were a gentleman—although you are quite about in your thinking to believe so—he might be tempted to take even more liberties than an ordinary farmer might."

"Are you saying that he *is* a gentleman, papa?" Susannah asked, her brown eyes wide.

"You are missing the point, Susannah," Lady Grainly said severely.

"Have you not been listening?" her father blustered on top of this. "I have repeatedly said that he was *not*."

"I see," Susannah said meekly, but she did not believe him, for she noticed how his mouth twitched, a sure sign he was not being completely open with her.

"Then that is settled," Sir Basil said, clearing his throat. "Now, lest you might think you will have a great deal of free time lying heavy on your hands because you will not be out and about as much as you are used, let me assure you that your grandmother and I have made provision for the useful employment of your leisure. Your grandmother wishes to finish off your education, to turn you into a young lady so that men like MacDougal will not go about mistaking you for a child any longer. You are to mind what she says. Is that understood, Susannah?"

"Yes, papa," she said, still intrigued by the possibility of Sandy's being a gentleman and not really attending to him.

"Indeed, I would like to begin on that project tomorrow," Lady Grainly said, "but we will be far too busy preparing for Lord Westbridge. I do, however, expect you to be on your best behavior before his lordship tomorrow night."

"Of course, grandmamma," Susannah said automatically.

"Your father and I wish you to make a good impression upon him; indeed, it is most important that you should do so, for reasons we will explain to you soon. You must mind your manners and curb your tongue. Is that quite clear, Susannah?"

"Yes, grandmamma."

"You may go now, Susannah."

"Yes, grandmamma."

"That was well done, Basil," Lady Grainly said once

Susannah had left them. "I must admit I did not think you had it in you to be so firm."

"On this point I am in complete agreement with you, mamma," Sir Basil said fervently.

However, if Lady Grainly thought they had succeeded in putting Sandy MacDougal out of Susannah's mind, she was much mistaken. If Susannah had thought often of him before, now she could think of nothing else. Sir Basil's hints only added to the mystery of Sandy's past and made him much more attractive to her. Would he actually take liberties with her if he knew she was old enough to receive them? What exactly *were* liberties? Holding her hand? He had done that today and it hadn't seemed wrongful at all; in fact, "brotherly" described the gesture more accurately. Would he try to kiss her? For some reason, Susannah was not shocked by such a notion but, rather, tingled with delight. She closed her eyes, trying to imagine what it would be like to feel his strong, sturdy arms about her, to feel his lips upon hers.

She was standing dreamily in the middle of her room, pretending she was locked in his embrace, when a knock came upon the door, and before waiting for a reply Lucy entered.

"What are you doing?" she inquired curiously, for Susannah appeared to be performing some strange dance.

"Nothing, just daydreaming," Susannah replied, putting her arms down hastily.

"You would do better to spend your time tidying up your room," Lucy said, picking up the riding skirt from the floor where Susannah had let it drop.

"What difference does it make? No one ever comes in here but you, and when you come in, you tidy it for me."

Lucy laughed as she shook out the skirt and hung it neatly on a peg in the wardrobe. "Yes, you have me well in hand, Sukey."

Susannah sat upon the bed and proceeded to remove her shoes and stockings. "You might mend these while you're about it. I have got another hole."

"Give it to me," Lucy said with a sigh. "I suppose I can do it while I am mending the tablecloth tomorrow. We would not want Lord Westbridge to see you with a hole in your stocking." She smoothed it out to examine the extent of the damage.

Susannah did not wish to speak about Lord Westbridge right now; she had heard enough about him at dinner and had other things on her mind at present. After regarding her aunt thoughtfully for a moment, she asked suddenly, "Aunt Lu, have you ever been kissed?"

Lucy looked up in horror at her niece, blushing to the roots of her hair. "Susannah! How could you ever ask me such a thing?"

Susannah nearly crowed with delight at her aunt's discomfiture. "You have! I can tell by your face. Tell me—what was it like?" she pleaded.

"Really, Susannah, one doesn't discuss— It is not proper . . . I could not possibly—"

"I promise I would never ever tell grandmamma, but I do so want to know. Is it anything like it is in the books?"

Reluctantly, Lucy smiled. "A little," she admitted. "Of course, I have only been kissed once, but it was very . . . nice."

Susannah scowled slightly. The word "nice" seemed inadequate to describe what must have been the experience of a lifetime. "Only nice? Nothing more?" she asked, determined to extract as much information as possible.

"Well, it was . . . pleasant," Lucy supplied.

"Then you enjoyed it?"

"Oh, yes, I enjoyed it well enough," she smiled.

"Who was it, Aunt Lu?" Susannah asked in an eager whisper. But now she had gone too far.

"*That* I shall never tell," Lucy said severely, adding, "and I hope that is an end to this entire discussion. I will have your stocking mended in time for you to dress for dinner tomorrow night." And with that, she left for her own bedchamber.

❧ CHAPTER FOUR ❧

"I SIMPLY DO not understand why we are going to so much trouble just for old Lord Westbridge," Susannah complained to her aunt as Lucy helped to fasten her into her finest gown, which was already much worn and very tight in the bodice. On a rare evening of entertainment such as this, Lady Grainly could not spare Trunkett from her side, so the two younger ladies did for each other.

"He is not *old*," Lucy objected quietly. "Why, he is only one year older than I."

Susannah was immediately contrite. "Aunt Lu, I did not mean to say *you* were old. I only meant old in the sense that we have known him for donkey's years and had him over to dinner any number of times, but never before has so much fuss and bother been made over it. It would make more sense if the duke were coming, too."

"I suppose as mamma has so little opportunity to

entertain, she wishes to make the most of this one,'' Lucy suggested, but she too was slightly puzzled by the unprecedented flurry of activity that had been put into motion that day. Not only had she been required to mend the tablecloth, but she helped Susannah take up all the carpets in the drawing room and beat them vigorously, polished the furniture as well as the fire irons until the whole room smelled of beeswax and lemon oil, and laid the table carefully so that any china that was chipped or cracked should not be found at his lordship's place. Indeed, Susannah had been so occupied herself that she had found no time that day to disobey her father by visiting the Lewis farm in order to tell Sandy that she must not visit him anymore. The only chance she had to go out-of-doors at all was when she was sent to find some flowers for the table.

''There!'' Lucy said with a sigh of relief as she managed to fasten the last hook on Susannah's gown. ''Now, do not breathe too deeply or eat too much for dinner, or you will burst out of it.''

Susannah regarded herself critically in the looking glass. ''I hate this old dress,'' she complained. ''Surely grandmamma must see that I need a new one.''

''Let me tidy your hair,'' Lucy said, ignoring her comment, for she knew as well as her niece that the likelihood of either of them receiving a new gown in the near future was practically nil.

Susannah sat down at her dressing table and allowed her aunt to arrange her hair smoothly on top of her head.

''Of course, I am longing to see Lord Westbridge,'' she remarked, ''if only to discover whether the reports of his injuries have been greatly exaggerated.''

''I do hope you will not make a spectacle of yourself by

staring at him when he arrives,'' Lucy warned. ''It would be very rude.''

''You need not worry about that, Aunt Lu, for I am absolutely terrified of meeting his eyes, especially if they are both blackened. I know I should simply burst into gales of laughter should he fix me with that solemn gaze of his.''

''Then I suggest you keep your eyes demurely downcast, for it is not at all the thing to laugh at a guest.''

''If I *do* start laughing I will simply pretend that I need to be sick and run from the room!'' Susannah suggested brightly.

''Susannah! You must not do that!'' Lucy exclaimed, shocked. ''He would think there is something wrong with the food.''

''Then I will have a coughing fit—is that all right?'' She gazed at Lucy's image in the looking glass with such an expression of guileless innocence that Lucy was forced to laugh.

''Now I fear that if you so much as clear your throat, I will be unable to control myself,'' she said. ''There, you are finished. Just see if my sash is straight and we can go downstairs.''

Lucy's sash was straight and her hair tidy; indeed, she seemed to be in looks tonight. Her dress was as shabby and old as Susannah's, but fit her rather better, for she had not grown in the last three years, as Susannah had. The pink material was faded, but this more subdued shade was actually more flattering than the original bright hue, complementing the delicate flush on her normally pale cheeks, which caused Susannah to wonder if she had used paint.

Lady Grainly joined them in the drawing room a few minutes later, splendid in a royal blue silk gown of an earlier and wealthier time. She had chosen to wear the Grainly rubies tonight, and evidently Trunkett had spent the afternoon polishing them, for they glittered and sparkled magnificently. She lifted her eyeglass and gazed through it critically at her daughter and granddaughter.

"Well, I suppose that is the best we can do," she said with a small sigh as she regarded Lucy, then gave Susannah a more concentrated inspection. Her eyes glinted approvingly at the way the tight bodice emphasized the girl's blossoming bustline, and how the too-short skirt revealed a pair of neatly turned ankles.

"Susannah, do try to keep your right side turned away from Lord Westbridge," she directed, dropping the glass, "so that he will not notice that stain on your skirt."

"If I had a new dress, I could turn any way I liked," Susannah countered.

"Nonsense. That dress is perfectly adequate. The material is the finest silk available—in point of fact, you cannot buy silk like that anymore. I remember the original gown it was made from—there were yards and yards of saffron silk, with a gold lace overdress. It was very becoming to me." The calculating gleam returned to her eye. "Perhaps there might be some extra material left for a new panel in the skirt. I will speak to Trunkett about it."

Susannah sighed and resigned herself to disappointment. She was not about to get a new gown this time, only another repair on the old one.

Sir Basil joined them all presently. "My, my, don't you all look fine? Westbridge will fancy himself to be in the finest London saloon, I'll wager."

Susannah did not understand the nervous looks he cast her way from time to time as they awaited his lordship's arrival. She thought perhaps one of her seams had come apart, so closely was he scrutinizing her, but when she self-consciously made a hasty check she did not find anything amiss, except for the obvious complaint that the gown was too small for her.

Lord Westbridge presented himself promptly and with all his customary dignity, despite his alarming appearance. Indeed, he looked as if he had met up with the wrong end of a horse; both his eyes were livid, and there was a large white plaster on the bridge of his nose. He was provided with refreshment and attempted to make some light small talk, but from both Lucy and Susannah he met with nothing more than monosyllabic replies; Lucy because she was trying very hard to pretend there was nothing unusual about his appearance in the least, and this monumental task took all her powers of concentration; Susannah because she knew if she expressed herself in anything more than a simple yes or no she would burst into laughter. However, Lady Grainly more than made up for the reticence of the younger ladies, asking after Lord Westbridge's family and commenting on the state of the weather. That she was not unaware of his disfigurement was made apparent only by the fact that she did not inquire after his health—that would have been too obvious a question.

A social disaster was narrowly averted when they all filed into the dining room. Susannah could not resist clearing her throat just once and managed to catch Lucy's eye as she did so. With an amazing display of courage, unusual in one generally so timid, Lucy did not even crack a smile.

They were pleased to learn over dinner that the duke and duchess would be returning to Westham Park with their younger children, Westbridge's half-brothers, in a month's time, as soon as the London season was over.

"Nor will they be visiting the seaside this year," Westbridge explained, "as my stepmother is expecting her confinement in September, as you probably know."

Lady Grainly was forced to admit that this was public knowledge, although no formal announcement had ever been made.

"If your stepmother is up to receiving visitors, I am sure that Susannah and Lucy will be pleased to bear her company," Lady Grainly suggested.

"Oh, Phoebe is always up to receiving visitors," Westbridge said with his first—and last—hint of a smile.

Lady Grainly frowned slightly as she noticed the trouble he seemed to have chewing his meat. She hoped he had not been given a piece of gristle; her portion was remarkably tender, considering the age of the sheep.

They went on to discuss various aspects of estate management and whether the duke planned to sponsor the annual fête on the church green as usual this year. Considering the indisposition of the duchess, there was a possibility he would not have the time to involve himself in any outside activities.

"Phoebe would not hear of the fête's being canceled on her account," Westbridge assured them. "She is like a child when it comes to things like that and hates to be disappointed."

"Then she bears her indisposition well?" Lady Grainly asked.

"She is as strong as a horse in that regard," Westbridge said.

This led quite naturally to a discussion of horse breeding in general and the Westham racing stable in particular. Westbridge was knowledgeable on the subject, although the breeding and racing of horses was really his father's great interest and not his own.

"I expect you will be visiting some of the local racing meets together this summer, Sir Basil," Westbridge said politely.

"I certainly hope so. I do enjoy them, even though I am no more than a spectator most of the time," he said cheerfully.

"And I certainly hope you will remain so," Lady Grainly said sharply. She did not care for any mention of horse racing, for it was only another form of gambling in her eyes and as such reminded her too painfully of Sir Roland's excesses.

Sir Basil chuckled, trying to save face after his mother's reproof. "My mother is afraid I will lose more than we can afford, but I only ever wager a crown at most. Indeed, your father usually advises me so well that I often come home as much as a pound richer than I left."

"And how is your sister, Lady Imogen?" Lady Grainly asked, forcefully steering the conversation away from all mention of wagers and winnings.

"She is well, thank you," Westbridge informed them. "She and her husband are planning a visit to Italy this summer."

"Then she will not be visiting with you at Westham?" she asked, and Westbridge shook his head. "That is too bad. We will miss her company. She is such a *vivacious* woman." She cast a pointed glance at Sir Basil, as much as to say, "So different from Fanny," but he missed it. "Does she not yet have any news of an interesting nature to relate?"

"Not yet," Westbridge said.

Lady Grainly nodded. Lady Imogen's childless state

was the only thing that softened her reproach toward her son for not marrying her. Fanny had failed to produce an heir, but Lady Imogen would have proved even more inconsiderate, by producing no offspring whatsoever.

Susannah was heartily bored by all this and wished they would talk about something *interesting,* such as the details of Westbridge's fight or a description of his jilting lover. She would also have liked to ask after his other sibling, Lord Ingram. She had only ever heard tantalizing hints about his story and would dearly love to be more completely informed on the matter. But the talk remained on horses and fêtes, the health of little lords Jasper and Leslie, which of the brood mares would produce a likely offspring, and how many sheep had been born that spring. Soon they would be getting to the cows and pigs, and probably even the chickens, Susannah thought with disgust. But she knew well that any efforts on her part to change the subject would be quashed without ceremony by her grandmother. She minded her manners and curbed her tongue, as she had been told, answering politely only when directly addressed.

At long last Lady Grainly nodded to her and Lucy that it was time to withdraw from the men.

"I certainly hope we don't make a habit of *that,*" Susannah said once in the drawing room, stretching her arms and nearly ripping out her sleeves in the process. She put her arms down quickly when she realized the danger. "I would rather have the duke for dinner, personally. He is so much more amusing. Don't you agree?"

"Lord Westbridge happens to be a very serious young man, which I find a great advantage in this day and age," Lady Grainly said severely. "Sit down, Susannah, and show some decorum. I should not like his lordship to find you doing calisthenics when he comes in with your father. Take an example from your aunt, please. Whatever her faults, she has always been able to sit quietly and occupy herself with some gentle pursuit.''

Lucy had taken up her needlework upon entering the drawing room and now flushed at this unexpected compliment, backhanded though it might have been. She so rarely won her mother's approval.

Susannah seated herself obediently and made a movement to open her workbox and take out some mending to occupy herself. This, too, was unacceptable to her grandmother.

''No, Susannah, better you should read a book of poetry than allow his lordship to discover you darning your undergarments.''

Susannah sighed and looked around, but there were no books at hand. ''Shall I fetch one from the library, grandmamma?'' she asked.

''That will not be necessary,'' Lady Grainly decided. ''I would rather you sat here and talked to me. Tell me, what did you think of Lord Westbridge?''

Susannah regarded her blankly for a moment. ''What did I think of Lord Westbridge?'' she repeated stupidly.

Lady Grainly sighed. ''Susannah, how often have I told you that to answer one question with another is very bad conversational practice? When someone asks you a question, you should answer directly and truthfully, perhaps adding some comment of your own afterwards to continue the conversation. Now, tell me. What did you think of Lord Westbridge?''

''I found him just as boring as ever I did,'' Susannah said directly and truthfully. ''He rather reminded me of that funny little bull terrier papa once had—do you remember it, grandmamma? It was all white with black circles around each eye. What *was* his name? Aunt Lu, do you remember?''

''I'm afraid not,'' Lucy said with a nervous glance at her mother, who was not pleased with this turn in the conversation Susannah had introduced.

''I shall ask papa when he comes in,'' Susannah decided, ''for I shall lie awake all night trying to think of it otherwise.''

''You will do nothing of the kind!'' her grandmother exclaimed, horrified. ''Really, Susannah, I sometimes think it is just as well we could not afford to give you a London season. I have a dreadful feeling you would have disgraced yourself entirely. Please do not make any comments of that nature to Lord Westbridge.''

''Whyever should I want to talk about papa's dogs with Lord Westbridge?'' Susannah asked. ''Although, I suppose he might be interested if they were bitches. He would want to know how well they are increasing.''

Lady Grainly saw nothing amusing in this remark and proceeded to read Susannah a lengthy lecture on what was proper conversational material for a young lady and a young gentleman. Fortunately, this was cut short when Sir Basil and Lord Westbridge joined them.

The look Sir Basil and his mother exchanged was not lost on Susannah, and she wondered if her father had finally decided to sell that bit of land the duke had wanted for so long. If his slight nod meant that he had been successful, perhaps this evening's boredom would not have been for nothing and might be worth at least a new gown. Westbridge himself seemed to be quite cheerful, and even graced her with a rare smile. However, Susannah was not to learn the subject of their discussion tonight, for Westbridge soon took his leave and she was sent off to bed, but not before she discovered that the name of Sir Basil's terrier had been Bull's-Eye. She considered it a perfect sobriquet for Westbridge himself.

After breakfast the next morning, Susannah received a summons to wait upon her father in the estate office. She searched her conscience guiltily, trying to discover any infraction of the rules she might have committed since his last lecture and for once felt confident that so far she was blameless. Surely he could not have guessed her intention of visiting the Lewis farm that morning—and it was only a short visit she had planned, after all. No, Trunkett's roving eye must have discovered some other sin she had unknowingly committed, and reported faithfully to her grandmother.

"Susannah, sit down. I wish to talk to you," Sir Basil greeted her after she had knocked and been invited to enter.

She had to move the estate map from the chair before she could obey him and was surprised to notice how her hands were shaking. Sir Basil was usually so cheerful and affectionate with her when he was outside his mother's influence, but today he was so serious that Susannah wondered if something dreadful had happened. She had not yet seen her grandmother that morning, but Lady Grainly was habitually a late riser. Surely she could not have had an attack during the night without Susannah's hearing the commotion.

She sat down and folded her hands neatly on her lap, waiting for her father to speak.

"My dear Susannah," he began, then paused for a deep breath. "You know that our financial situation has never been very good since your grandfather gambled away our fortune."

"Of course I know that, papa," she said, puzzled that he should state such an obvious circumstance of their lives. "I have not been overspending my pin money, if that is what you are worried about."

"No, no, I know you have not," he said, "though you get little enough as it is. Nor have you complained about all the nice things you might have were we not so poor."

"Well, it *would* be nice to have some new clothes, but then as long as I have my pony, there is little else I desire," she told him reassuringly. Suddenly, her face fell. "Oh, papa, you are not going to sell Bessy, are you? She does not eat very much, and I have always taken good care of her. Whatever should I do without her?"

"No, it is not that, Susannah," he said. "I would not sell Bessy. Indeed, she is worth more to you than any money I could get for her." He ran his hand through his hair. "As we told you the other night, Susannah, your grandmother wishes to finish off your education. It now appears that the process must be considerably speeded up."

"Yes, papa," she said. She was still totally bewildered and had no idea what he was leading to.

"You see, I—that is, your grandmother and I—have been exploring ways of increasing our capital." He shook his head and indicated his ledger, the bottle of red ink sitting upon it. "This inflation has been eating away what little we had left. I do not like to worry you about such things, but you must understand that since the war everything has been increasing in price, while our income has remained the same. This, naturally, adds to our deficits."

Susannah creased her brow, trying to determine why he was telling her this. She was well aware of their poverty; indeed, she had been brought up in it. "Do you want me to go to work, papa?'' she asked. ''I would be pleased to if it would help you at all. Perhaps I could get a situation as a governess somewhere. I know I am a trifle young for that, but I do like children and—''

''No, that will not be necessary,'' he interrupted. ''I *had* been thinking about approaching the heir, but you must have heard what happened when I made that suggestion.''

Susannah rolled her eyes expressively. ''Lucy told me all about it,'' she said. ''Indeed, I was surprised to hear you had been so bold, papa, knowing the effect it must have on grandmamma's heart.'' There was a note of reproach in her voice.

''That I *did* risk the suggestion, knowing the probable outcome, must illustrate to you the gravity of our situation.''

''Yes, papa,'' Susannah said.

''Happily,'' he said, introducing a lighter note to his words, ''your grandmother and I have hit upon a much more acceptable solution to our financial problems, but it is a solution that needs your approval as well, Susannah.''

She regarded him curiously, quite unprepared to guess what this solution might be. ''Well?'' she prompted after a moment's silence.

Sir Basil took a deep breath. ''What do you think of Lord Westbridge?'' he asked.

Susannah wondered why everyone seemed so interested in her opinion of Lord Westbridge lately, and what the opinion had to do with the finances of Birchwood Hall. Indeed, her father was regarding her anxiously now, as if everything depended upon her reply to that question.

''What do I think of Lord Westbridge?'' she repeated slowly.

Sir Basil read her no lecture on her conversational habits but prompted, ''Do you find him agreeable? Congenial?

Do you admire his virtues? Approve of his tastes? In short, do you think you and he would suit?''

Susannah swallowed the lump that had formed in her throat as the reason for his questions became clear to her. "Grandmamma wishes me to marry Lord Westbridge?'' she asked in wonder.

"We both do,'' Sir Basil assured her, then continued rapidly. "We want above all things to see that you are well provided for—for the rest of your life. Any short-term solution to our financial woes would not allow for what will happen to you once I am gone, but if you were to marry Westbridge, your grandmother and I could both go to our graves with peace of mind, knowing that you will be taken care of for all of your life—indeed, that you will be a duchess one day.''

"But papa, you are not going to die for a great many years,'' Susannah protested.

"I certainly hope not,'' he agreed with a slight smile. "But still, one must make provisions. What if I were to have an accident out riding tomorrow? These things must be thought of, however distasteful that task must seem.''

"And what does Westbridge think of the idea?'' she asked in a small voice.

"He was most enthusiastic about it,'' Sir Basil assured her readily. "Indeed, he told me it was the answer to a prayer. He found you to be a most civil and presentable young lady and desired me to tell you that he would be most honored should you decide to share his life at Westham Park. Even your extreme youth weighed in your favor, as he indicated quite plainly he was weary of the bold, headstrong ladies he met with in London and would welcome a young, docile wife who would be content with remaining in the country and looking after her family.''

"It sounds as if he wants not a wife but a lapdog who can be trained to sit and beg and stay and heel," Susannah said with a sniff.

"My dear, you are old enough to see the necessity of such an alliance and young enough to change your ways to suit your husband," he told her sternly. "Come, now, Susannah, you have always been a favorite of the duke's. I know you would be welcomed warmly into the family."

"Yes, I like the duke much better than I like Westbridge," Susannah admitted. "And I like the duchess, too—she is such a dear little thing, but Lady Imogen and I have never got along well."

"Lady Imogen has her own house, and you would not see all that much of her," Sir Basil pointed out. He softened and tried to smile, but his mouth was twitching. "Susannah, dearest, I will not ask for your reply this minute. I ask you only to think over all the advantages that would be yours and remind you that any monies he should settle on you are sorely needed here. He will be coming to tea this afternoon to speak to you himself. Perhaps it would be a good idea if you took the intervening hours to think things over carefully. Go and have your ride, if that will do the trick—I see that you are dressed for it."

"Yes, papa, I will think it over," Susannah said numbly, rising.

Sir Basil arose, too, and came out from behind his desk to embrace her warmly.

"My little Sukey," he said tenderly, caressing her hair. "I cannot lie to you—I am not at all fond of the idea myself. To me you are still my little baby girl and always will be, and it is not easy for me to give you away in marriage. But I cannot think only of myself in this matter. I must think of your future, too. I doubt that an opportunity as wonderful as this will come along again. We must seize it while we can. Westbridge is a very wealthy man, and when he becomes duke he will be wealthier still; I know he will always be able to take good care of you. After all, it is not as though we were sending you off to strangers, far from your home; we have known the Westhams all our lives. Indeed, this will not be the first union between our two families.'' He chuckled slightly. ''For your dowry the Grainlys lose nothing—we are merely returning what once belonged to the Westhams.''

Susannah managed a faint smile. ''Do you mean the Fifty Acres? The duke will be pleased to get them back.''

''There, you see, yet another person who will be made happy by your marriage,'' Sir Basil said, ''to say nothing of your grandmother, who is in absolute raptures over the idea.'' He patted her again, then released her awkwardly. ''Now you go and think about whether *you* can be happy with it.''

''Very well, papa. I will,'' Susannah said.

Indeed, she wanted nothing more than to go off alone on her pony and think things over. This morning she had awakened with nothing more serious on her mind than whether she could find a pair of whole stockings to wear; by this afternoon she must decide her entire future. And it was not only her own future that was at stake but the fate of Birchwood Hall itself—this match had not been arranged for her benefit alone. *She* would be content to live out her life as she always had—poor but respectable, happy in her shabby clothes, content with the freedom their lack of resources had given her.

The choice was hers, her father had said, but she knew well this was not true. She had no choice in the matter; she would never be forgiven for refusing. A hundred times a day her grandmother would remind her of her stubbornness in her subtle, needling way. Dear me, she would sigh, if only we had the money for some new draperies, or if only we could afford a decent cut of meat once in a while. Then she would look at Susannah with reproach, her heartfelt sigh saying louder than words, If you had only been a dutiful child things would be very different.

But her grandmother's reproach would be nothing compared to the disgust she would feel for herself every time she met Lucy's eye as she was darning a stocking, or saw her father ride out on his old, spavined horse. Until now their poverty had been only her grandfather's fault and was as such easily accepted. If it continued, however, the fault would be on her head. She knew she could not live out her life under such a burden of blame.

Unconsciously, she had been leading her pony down the path that led to the Lewis farm, searching for a patch of red hair in the green fields, but she arrived at the very doorstep of his cottage without finding him. Why did he have to go to market on this day of all days, she thought resentfully, on this day, when she needed his friendship more than ever before. She almost cried with disappointment when she could not find him, and would even have gone into his cottage to wait had she not been worried that Bessy would be recognized and her grandmother would somehow hear of her forbidden visit. Even now Trunkett might be lurking behind that thicket, her wandering eye circling in mad opposition to its mate, recording anything that might be of interest to her mistress.

Susannah turned her pony away and headed in the direction of the Fifty Acres. She had a sudden desire to see the lands that would be her dowry, as if seeing them might make this whole nightmare real for her.

Why had *she* been given this responsibility? she thought as a feeling of anger began to percolate through her numbness. Why must *she* be the one to marry without love, without even liking, to pay for the sins of her grandfather, committed long before she was even born? She had not even been consulted beforehand, but the burden had been thrust upon her, full-blown, with no warning. It was beastly—no, it was worse than that; it was hateful! Unconscionable! Iniquitous!

She dismounted and tethered Bessy to a tree, suddenly desirous for an increased activity, to suit her present state of turmoil. She strode forcefully through the woods, swishing her riding crop viciously at any stray branch that blocked her progress. Finally she came across one that refused to budge, and she hit it repeatedly, harder and harder.

"Damn!" she burst out. "Damn papa! Damn grand-mamma! Damn Westbridge to hell!"

At last the offending limb could withstand no more punishment and fell off.

"Hout na!" cried a voice. "I'll stand sae much but naught mair! Troth, ye hae put me in fear o' my puir life."

"Sandy!" Susannah cried, and a mingled rush of joy and relief swept through her. "Oh, Sandy, whatever shall I do?" She flung herself into his arms, and as she was made welcome there she burst into tears.

❧ CHAPTER FIVE ❧

"Now, now, lassie," he said in a gentler accent, holding her tight as she sobbed against him. "Calm yourself, child. Surely it is not as bad as all that."

At last she seemed to be recovering and fumbled for a handkerchief to dry her eyes. Sandy released her gently, and bent to retrieve the riding crop she had dropped upon seeing him.

"I'm wonderin' if I dare return this to you," he said, hoping to jolly her out of her distress. "Have I your word you'll na be usin' this implement o' torture on my own poor pate?"

She smiled dismally. "Of course not, Sandy, it is not you I am angry with."

He made an exaggerated sigh of relief as he handed the crop back to her. "I'm thankful that my name isna

Westbridge, then, for if your recent invectives are any indication, you are sore angry wi' him.''

At the mention of Westbridge's name, Susannah once again renewed her sobs. ''Oh, Sandy, whatever shall I do?'' she wailed, seating herself upon a nearby boulder. By now her handkerchief was quite useless, so sodden had it become. Sandy sat next to her and offered his own; she took it and blew her nose loudly. This made her feel better.

''Now then,'' he said when he saw she was once more in a condition to speak coherently. ''Do you want to tell me what this is aboot, or is it none o' my business?''

''We had Westbridge for dinner last night,'' Susannah began darkly.

''I see! Then 'tis naught more than a spot o' indigestion that's troublin' you! I hadna realized, though, that things had come to such a pass at the Hall that you have taken to eatin' your neighbors.''

As was intended, this drew a laugh from Susannah, but it was a short-lived one at best.

''Come now, lassie,'' Sandy prompted, ''what has this Westbridge done that was so terrible you wished to damn him to hell at the top o' your lungs? Surely he's as good a Christian soul as you or I and should be allowed the possibility of an eternal reward as well as any other man.''

But Susannah was no longer in a mood to respond to his jocularity. Instead, she looked at him woefully and announced in tragic tones, ''Westbridge wishes to marry me.''

If she had wanted to draw a spectacular response from him, she had certainly succeeded.

''What? Is the man daft?'' he exclaimed, disbelieving.

''Apparently, none of the ladies in London suited his

taste, so he has turn his sights closer to home," Susannah explained with another little sniff into the handkerchief.

"But you're nae more than a bairn," he said, aghast. "Ah, I see it now—you're havin' a little bit o' fun wi' me," he finished hopefully.

"No, indeed," she assured him, "he and papa have worked it all out between them. The final decision rests with me, but it does not seem that I really have much choice. You see, we need the money very badly. There is something called inflation that worries papa terribly, and it is easy enough for me to see for myself that the house is falling to bits. I should never be able to look any of them in the face again if I refused."

"And how do they expect you, a mere child, to know what to do in a matter as grave as this?" he exclaimed angrily. "Your father must be daft as well to agree to such a thing. You are far too young to marry at all. Why, there must be laws against it, and by God if there are I'll make sure this is one case that will stand by those laws."

Her heart surged to hear him take her part so forcefully, yet she had small hope he could do anything about it. She lifted her brown eyes to him regretfully. "I am quite sure there are no such laws, Sandy, nor would such a marriage be at all unusual. I will be eighteen in two months' time— quite old enough to marry."

"Eighteen?" Sandy repeated, thunderstruck by this information. "But your own father told me himself you were nae more than thirteen."

"Papa tends to lose track of things like that," Susannah said with a shrug.

He rose and took a few steps away, then turned back to regard her once more, trying to seek the truth of her statement in her slender form. Certainly, she looked no more than thirteen, with her hair hanging loosely down her back and her childish clothing. She was such a tiny thing, too, and so ingenuous and uninhibited, not at all stiff and missish as he found other young ladies of her age to be. He could not accustom himself to the idea that she was a young woman, fully grown; it was too much for him to take in so quickly. Had he known her true age from the beginning he would have behaved quite differently toward her. He would not have allowed her to see him working in his shirtsleeves, or invited her into his homely cottage, where the bed was often left unmade. He would have kept his distance, been more respectful, tried to keep in mind that he was a tenant and she a lady.

"Sandy, what should I do?" she asked again quietly.

"I dinna see there's ought ye can do, miss," he said, lapsing back into his thicker accent as if it were a refuge.

"Then you think I should marry him?"

"Ye haena much choice, hae ye?" He was beginning to feel angry again. What right had she to question him thus, as though he had the power to do anything about it? Sir Basil and that mother of his had worked it all out between them; it had nothing to do with *him*.

"But I am not even certain I *like* him, let alone—anything else." She could not bring herself to mention the word love in connection with Westbridge; it seemed somehow blasphemous.

Sandy fell back on his Scots practicality. "They do say some o' the best marriages are built on little mair than that, miss."

"Can't you help me, Sandy?" Her tear-stained face was stricken.

"Nae, I canna!" he burst out furiously.

She reacted to his angry tone as if she had been slapped. "Then what should I do?" she cried out desperately.

"Ye'll marry his lairdship and be happy to do it! Troth, child, yer family hoose is fallin' doon, the fences need repair, twa farms are lyin' fallow because there are nae funds t' repair the cottages for new tenants. Acres o' guid grazin' land are empty o' a' livestock but the wee field mice and rabbits. Ye ken weel enow this marriage isna for yer sake alone. Indaid, ye shad be grateful t' yer father for arrangin' such a fine match. Miss," he added at the last.

Susannah could not quite believe that the Sandy Mac-Dougal who had been her friend and confidant was one and the same as this angry, stomping Scotsman she now saw before her, who spoke in a burr so thick she could hardly understand him. Yet she understood enough to realize that he, too, was willing to sacrifice her for the sake of Birchwood Hall. And why not? He was a tenant; he would profit by Westham monies as well, perhaps in the shape of a new fence or repairs to his cottage. She had been a fool indeed to think he could offer her sympathy and understanding. For once her grandmother was right—it did not do to go gossiping with servants or making friends of them; they were incapable of feeling the deeper emotions and would turn on you as soon as look at you.

She stood up and shook out her skirts with as much dignity as she could muster.

"I don't suppose I'll be seeing you again, MacDougal," she said, her head held proudly. "My father has forbidden me to visit you and I see now that he was right."

He accepted this with no demur. "Quite right, miss, tha's ha it shad be. The likes o' ye ought hae naught t' do wi' the likes o' me. I wish ye happy on yer weddin' day, miss," he finished, pulling his forelock respectfully.

She was about to turn and walk back to where she had tethered Bessy, but almost inadvertently, a cry came out, "Doesn't it make any difference to you at all? Doesn't our friendship mean anything to you? Are you content to see me enter a loveless marriage? Even to give it your blessing?"

": 'Tis naught t' do wi' me, miss," he said politely but coldly.

She gave him one last, heartrending gaze, then squared her shoulders and walked away without looking back. If she had, she might have been surprised to see him standing as she left him, watching her progress until she was hidden by the bushes and leaves. She would have been even more surprised had she still been in earshot when he pounded his fist into the other hand and exclaimed,

"By God, there *is* something I can do! Basil Grainly will be called to account for this one, and soon!"

Lord Westbridge arrived at Birchwood Hall on the stroke of three, precisely the time he had been asked for. To Susannah, who had now resigned herself to the inevitable, this promptness could be seen as a great virtue in a future husband. Apparently, he was not reluctant to see her again and press his suit, or he might have been late; on the other hand, he was not overtaken by a loverlike eagerness, which would have made him early. He was prompt; that much and no more could be said of him.

He was shown into the drawing room, where Susannah, Lucy, and Lady Grainly all awaited him. Simons then shambled off to the estate office to tell Sir Basil that his guest had arrived.

Westbridge greeted them each in turn, formally and in strict order of precedence. When he reached Susannah's side at last, she had already had time to notice that he had removed the plaster from his nose and no longer resembled quite so vividly the little dog Sir Basil had once owned. Any inclination she had had to laugh yesterday had completely deserted her by now, and so intent was she in cataloguing the good points of her soon-to-be betrothed that her demeanor was quite serious and intent, both attributes Westbridge valued greatly in his future bride.

Indeed, Ivor could hardly believe his good fortune. A scant forty-eight hours ago he had been a broken man, jilted and wounded, ashamed to face his father in his disgrace. Now he was betrothed again—or nearly so—and the process had been so quick and painless, requiring so little effort on his part that he was disposed to be kindly to all the world. He could even find it in his heart to forgive Miss Durant, Jezebel that she was, for he was rapidly discovering that Miss Grainly outshone his former lover on every point, excepting perhaps intelligence and wit—both of which he had learned were of no value whatsoever in a prospective bride. Furthermore, he was now looking forward to bringing his father the good news about the return of the Fifty Acres. Indeed, so pleased was he with his choice (quite forgetting that the entire idea had come from Sir Basil) that he was quite prepared to make certain his father was extremely generous in the marriage settlement.

Sir Basil was not long in joining them, and soon after him arrived Simons with the tea cart. Lady Grainly invited them all to be seated as she poured the tea, and Susannah handed out the cups and served the portions of bread and butter. The conversation was much as it had been the night before, the only difference being Westbridge's tendency to smile a great deal more than usual, and Susannah a great deal less.

Finally, Sir Basil put down his empty cup and, with a

hollow chuckle, claimed pressing duties that needed his immediate attention. He gave both Susannah and Westbridge a number of significant glances, but no more than would naturally be expected of an anxious father on the verge of giving away his only daughter's hand. Shortly thereafter, Lady Grainly requested Lucy's attendance with her on some domestic matter, and if Lucy had not already been informed about what was to take place between the two people thus left alone in the room, she would have been surprised at her mother's sudden interest in her opinion on a domestic matter of any kind.

Thus Susannah was, for the first time, alone with Lord Westbridge, and quite at a loss as to what she should say to him.

He had arisen when the other two ladies exited and now turned to Susannah. "Miss Grainly," he began, then put a hand briefly to his forehead, a feeling of dizziness coming upon him.

"Pray sit down again, my lord," Susannah invited, and she was about to make some sympathetic comment about his injuries but thought such a remark might be too personal, considering their brief acquaintance.

He sat down heavily and Susannah waited patiently until his dizziness had passed.

"Miss Grainly," he repeated at last, "I will come straight to the point. Last night your father and I had quite an interesting talk. You cannot be fully ignorant of what it was we spoke about."

"No indeed," she admitted, wishing he would hurry and get it over with.

"We have both agreed that it would be to our mutual benefit were you and I to make a match of it," he said, then smiled. "All that is needed to seal the bargain is your approval."

Susannah could not imagine a more ungraceful proposal. It was not what she had expected, even coming from Lord Westbridge, but she knew she must be satisfied, for she would not receive another.

She took a deep breath, prepared to do her duty. "Certainly I approve, my lord."

"Then you will marry me?" he asked, not eagerly as a lover might, but as if he wanted to be quite certain there was no misunderstanding between them.

"Yes, my lord," she replied.

He heaved a great sigh and Susannah fully expected to hear him say, Thank God that's done, for it was obvious that was what he was thinking. However, he did seem to have some knowledge of the conventions of the situation, for he said, somewhat awkwardly, "I need not tell you how happy that makes me, Miss Grainly. Or may I call you Susannah now?"

"If we are engaged it would be entirely appropriate, my lord," she told him.

"Then you must call me Ivor, Susannah."

"Of course, Ivor," she repeated dutifully, uttering his Christian name only with difficulty.

He stood up and held out his hand to her. Susannah was not quite certain what was required at this point but arose and took it hesitantly. For a brief, panic-stricken moment she was afraid he was going to kiss her, and she knew she would have to submit to such an embrace, indeed, that it would only be the first in a lifetime of such attentions. So she steeled herself to receive the touch of his lips with fortitude, only to be spared this ordeal for the time being when he merely gave her hand a brief squeeze and dropped

73

it again. Despite her trepidation, she was slightly disappointed. Then she realized that any misplaced pressure on his face might cause his wounds to ache anew and he was simply being careful, not cold.

"I shall be remaining in the country for another week at the least," he told her, more at ease now that the business of their betrothal had been taken care of. "I hope to see you frequently during that time. We must learn to know one another better, Susannah."

"Of course, Ivor," she agreed. "Will you be returning to London then?"

"Only for the end of the season," he said, "I expect I will summer here, with my father and stepmother. We will have plenty of time to make more detailed arrangements for our wedding then."

They both sat down again, each casting about for ways to continue the conversation so they would not be forced to sit in total silence. Somehow, it did not seem appropriate that Westbridge should take his leave quite so soon; yet there seemed no reason for him to stay.

"I had an idea we might honeymoon in the south," he said presently. "I should like to visit Spain again, and I have never been to the south of France or to Italy. Would you like that, Susannah?"

"Certainly, my l—— Ivor," she replied.

Her quiet complaisance pleased him, and he was more than satisfied that at last he had found himself the correct wife. She was young enough that he could mold her to his ways rather than otherwise, and if her quietness of manner was due rather to stupidity than to shyness, that too was no drawback. At least she had the promise of great beauty and would look well at his side. Even if she never opened her mouth, she would do him credit.

At last a timid knock came upon the door, and Susannah called out, "Come in," rather more eagerly than might be expected of a young lady closeted alone with her betrothed.

Lucy entered with an apologetic air, mumbling something about a book her mother had left there. She finished off with an expectant look that revealed the true purpose of her errand.

"Aunt Lucy, Lord Westbridge has asked me to be his wife," Susannah said, and suddenly all the weight of the calamities of that day struck her forcibly, and murmuring a quick farewell to her husband-to-be she ran quickly up to her bedchamber, where she could give full vent to her tears.

Lucy watched her precipitous exit with surprise, then turned back to Ivor. "You must forgive my niece," she said. "She is young—I am sure she was simply overcome with emotion."

"Certainly," Ivor agreed. It was quite right and proper that a young lady could not contain herself after being asked to be *his* bride.

Lucy smiled shyly. "I suppose I will be your aunt now, Ivor," she said with amusement.

He answered her smile with a brief one of his own. "I should have expected as much—I already have a stepmother who is younger than I. But I do hope you will not require me to call you Aunt Lu, as Susannah does—it would be quite out of the question. Even Phoebe does not ask me to call her mamma."

Lucy laughed with appreciation at his little joke. "You may call me whatever you like, Ivor. I expect we will be seeing a great deal of you now that there is to be a permanent connection between our families."

"Only for the next week, or until my injuries have

healed more completely," he said, "then I will be returning to London for the rest of the season. I have some engagements there I cannot miss."

"I see," Lucy said, disappointed.

"But I will be returning to Westham Park in July," he assured her. "By the end of the summer I'll wager you will be glad to see the back of me."

"Certainly not, Ivor. You know you would always be welcome here, even if you were not marrying Susannah." She flushed slightly, although her remarks had not really exceeded the bounds of common civility. "Indeed, I must admit I am glad for a reason for more comings and goings between our two houses. We have been very quiet here."

"That would explain why Susannah is so shy," Westbridge said. "She must be little used to company."

"Susannah shy?" Lucy asked, amazed.

"Certainly," he said, wondering that she should think otherwise. "She has hardly uttered more than five words consecutively to me. But I am confident that both you and Phoebe will be able to bring her out of her shell. That is, if she is not lacking in wit."

"I assure you, Ivor, she has fully as many wits as you could desire."

"Good," he said seriously, "although I am surprised to hear it. One would have thought she would be more outgoing, especially with your example to follow."

Lucy was amused by this picture of herself and her niece, which was quite contrary to the truth. "Of course, Susannah does not know you very well yet," she pointed out, "whereas you and I grew up together. Although I must admit that in recent years I felt we had lost the familiarity of our youth." She was surprised at her own boldness but gratified that Ivor took it in part.

"If there was any loss of familiarity or friendship, obviously the fault was mine," he said gallantly, "for you remain as gentle and well-spoken as ever you were. In future, I hope we can become friends again, Lucy, as we once were."

"That would please me very much," she told him, and when she smiled this time her face lit up so that she appeared almost pretty.

❦ CHAPTER SIX ❧

LORD WESTBRIDGE REMAINED in the country for another week and a half, during which time he visited Birchwood Hall daily. Always considerate of the Grainlys' difficult financial situation and mindful, too, of his still tender jaw and delicate digestion, he carefully timed his visits so they would not coincide with mealtimes at the Hall. Thus, if he called in the morning, he left well before luncheon; if he called in the afternoon it was usually to take Susannah and Lucy for a drive, and he would leave them at the door without entering the house himself, even if they pressed him to stay for tea. Lady Grainly did invite him to dinner several nights after the first occasion, but he refused, claiming that he was in no position to return the invitation while only he was in residence at Westham, and if he fingered his jaw in painful remembrance while making this refusal, at least he was not so rude as to speak aloud his distaste for mutton.

In the short space of a few days Susannah's life changed so radically that she hardly had time to regret old friends. Her grandmother began her intensive training program immediately, and the new duties imposed on her left Susannah little time for reflection.

In the mornings, before Westbridge's visit, the lesson was usually deportment. Susannah was required to circumnavigate the drawing room with a volume of Dr. Johnson's dictionary perched upon her head. Lady Grainly had been trained in this same manner in her youth, and while fashion no longer dictated that ladies should wear great wigs sporting birds' nests or the Spanish armada, the heaviness of the book was nonetheless valuable in helping to achieve the careful bearing and uplifting of carriage so desirable in a young lady.

After their light noonday meal came the music lessons. A tuner had been called in for the harpsichord, much to Lucy's delight and Susannah's dismay. Susannah much preferred the sound of a pianoforte, although she could not play one of those either, and joined in with the tuner when he tried to convince Lady Grainly to buy the more modern instrument.

"Certainly not," Lady Grainly had told them both severely. "There is already a pianoforte at Westham Park that you will soon be able to use, Susannah."

"But we should have one of our own," Susannah said, more for Lucy's sake than her own—her aunt had positively lit up when the suggestion was made. "A harpsichord is simply not fashionable anymore."

"We have not the money for it, and there is an end to it," Lady Grainly said, unwilling to submit this argument to the tuner, who would doubtless spread her remark over the entire county by nightfall, but even more unwilling to give in on an item so frivolous. Had she the money to spend on a piano, she would not spend it on a piano, she stated firmly, and no one dared dispute her logic.

Susannah was expected to practice at least an hour a day upon the harpsichord, and if this was sheer torture for her to perform, she was consoled by the knowledge that it must have been even more painful for her grandmother to hear. It gave her much more pleasure to sit by while Lucy played, and perhaps join in with a song, but nothing would satisfy Lady Grainly except that her granddaughter should be able to accompnay herself as any young lady of quality was expected to do. Fortunately, Susannah was not yet required to perform for Lord Westbridge and hoped fervently that she would improve so little as to never have to perform for him.

Then came instruction in fine needlework, another bane to Susannah's peace and happiness. She was set to make a sampler of her grandmother's design, one she thought to be tasteless and garish in the extreme. However, as most of her time was spend untangling knots or undoing stitches that did not pass Lady Grainly's careful inspection, she was relieved to know the piece was never likely to be completed and displayed, so hers were the only sensibilities that would be offended by the sight of a purple butterfly alighting on a crimson flower.

Dancing was rather an easier accomplishment for Susannah to master, as she had a natural grace and a good memory for the intricate patterns of the country dances. She did rather better than Lucy at this pursuit, for besides being rusty at the dances, Lucy was required to stand in as Susannah's partner and often forgot exactly which way she should be going. Lady Grainly tapped out a rhythm with her walking stick as she intoned, "da *da* da da, da *da* da da," and each time Lucy missed a step the cane came crashing down with a thunderous clap as she cried out, "No *no,* Lucy, you silly girl! How is Susannah ever to learn if you continue to trip her up?"

"Perhaps we could ask Simons to help," Susannah suggested at last when one of Lucy's missteps proved particularly painful, but this idea did not suit her grandmother at all.

"What would Simons know of dancing?" Lady Grainly said with a fine disdain. "He is a servant."

"The servants dance during the holidays," Susannah pointed out. "Besides that, Simons is nearly as tall as Lord Westbridge, and it would help me to become accustomed to his lordship's unusual height."

"There is nothing unusual about Ivor's height," Lucy protested. "It is you who are unusually short."

"Perhaps *you* don't find him too tall, Aunt Lu, but then you are tall yourself. You probably don't think Simons tall either."

"Girls, I will have no more of this," Lady Grainly interrupted. "Height should not matter if one is an accomplished dancer. Now, Lucy, do try to concentrate. Da *da* da da, da *da* da da."

At least Lucy was allowed to rest while Susannah was drilled on points of etiquette and behavior in the fashionable world. This reminded her painfully of childhood lessons with her governess; learning the finer points of precedence was very like memorizing dates from history, and modes of behavior in town life, as recalled by her grandmother, seemed quite as exotic and foreign to Susannah as the fashions and mores of ancient Rome, and quite as useless.

Lady Grainly was soon satisfied that her program was working. Susannah displayed a new quietness of manner and a willing obedience that she had never shown before. That this new attitude might be attributable to some trouble of mind the girl was suffering and not the success of the intensive training was not a possibility that occurred to Lady Grainly. If it had, she would have dismissed it with a decisive "faugh!" What could there be to trouble the girl, after all? She was making a brilliant match with a most handsome and well-spoken gentleman, and she would live in luxury until the end of her days. Lady Grainly recalled the innocent happiness she had known during her own period of betrothal to Sir Roland and did not see any reason that her granddaughter should not be experiencing the same rapture even now. Indeed, her pleasure must be even greater, for there could be no disquieting periods of foreboding in it—Lord Westbridge was not a man to waste his inheritance at the gaming table. He would husband his resources well and see to it that his wife and children never wanted for anything. Yes, Susannah was a very lucky girl indeed, Lady Grainly decided, and was not loath to take full credit for this luck.

The only break in their new routine came on the day Lady Grainly announced that her joints were not aching as much as usual and might even carry her comfortably through a session with the dressmaker. Now that she had the opportunity to observe her granddaughter closely on a daily basis, she finally noticed how shabby and ill-fitting all her clothes were and decided that the time had come to do something about it.

Naturally, the news of Susannah's betrothal to Lord

Westbridge had become common knowledge in Duxtonbury less than an hour after it had taken place, due to the efficiency of the Duxtonbury news network. Mrs. Maggins had been looking forward to this visit from the Grainlys. If credit had been tight before in her dealings with the Hall, she was now more than eager to extend any courtesy possible to the future duchess of Duxton, confident that from now on she and all her family would be buying much more than darning cotton from her.

The three ladies were made welcome and invited into the private parlor behind the shop, where Lady Grainly was seated majestically in a place of honor from which she could view all the proceedings with ease. Mrs. Maggins spread out a number of fashion plates for their perusal and sent her sewing girls back and forth to fetch bolts of figured muslin and watered silk and display any number of laces and trims.

"I can make you up anything as fine as you would find in London," she assured them modestly. "My girls here all sew beautifully—and quick, too. I can deliver at least two day dresses and an evening dress within a week for each of the young ladies."

Lady Grainly had not considered any new clothing for Lucy—what she had fit well enough. At length, however, she allowed herself to be persuaded, especially after she recalled that she would not be the one to foot the bill for it all. She drew the line at any new garments for herself, however.

"My lady, I have a ruby satin that would be splendid with your white hair," Mrs. Maggins said, unwilling to give up the attempt without a struggle and clicking her fingers at one of the girls to bring this satin forth for display.

"I do not care for the newer fashions," Lady Grainly declared. "I find them indecent and decadent. Were I to visit London, which my health certainly does not permit, I might be tempted to order a new gown or two, but only from my own dressmaker in that great city."

Mrs. Maggins had to satisfy herself with the orders for the two younger ladies, which were quite enough to keep her and her girls busy for many weeks to come. In addition to two new evening dresses and four day dresses for each of them, Susannah insisted upon a new riding habit in a beautiful amber-brown serge, which Mrs. Maggins proposed to trim with brown velvet. She also ordered all manner of undergarments and accessories—little lace gloves that would be dyed to match each dress, delicate satin slippers, and beaded reticules. And on that very day they took away with them Mrs. Maggins's entire stock of silk stockings. Susannah added to their purchases with a grim determination, keeping in mind that this was why she was marrying Westbridge in the first place—so Lucy would never have to mend another stocking.

What with all her lessons and Westbridge's frequent visits, Susannah had little time to ride out on her pony as she used to, and when she did manage to squeeze a ride in after breakfast she felt no inclincation to disobey her father by visiting a certain Scottish tenant. Indeed, every time her thoughts strayed reluctantly toward the Lewis farm—which was far more often than she wished them to—she felt a sick feeling of betrayal in the pit of her stomach. It was best to forget her former childhood associations completely, Susannah told herself firmly, the same day she carefully laundered the pocket handkerchief he had lent her and put it away neatly in her linen press. He was not, could never be, a friend to her, she averred. He existed in a world quite different from her own. If she had only realized that sooner, she would have been spared a great deal of disappointment.

Several days later, Susannah decided she did not care to leave the handkerchief tucked away; it would be better to carry it with her in her pocket. Then should she chance to meet its owner on one of her rides—an unlikely possibility but a possibility nonetheless—she could return it to him at once. Of course, it was highly unlikely that she *would* meet him, nor did she wish to; but still . . . it was best to have the thing handy, or he might flatter himself by thinking she had kept it as a memento.

She considered herself completely cured of any childish infatuation she might have felt for one S. MacDougal when she was able to express her newly revised opinion of him to her father one morning when he found her in the stable still giving Bessy her rubdown.

"You haven't been out to the Lewis farm?" he asked her point-blank.

"Indeed not, papa," she replied, hurt that he should mistrust her. "Why should you think such a thing? You were quite right about that man. He is an ill-educated brute, and I certainly want nothing more to do with him. How could you think I would visit him, especially against your wishes?"

He was somewhat taken aback by her vehemence. "Forgive me, Sukey. I did not mean to doubt you," he said.

"Very well, papa," she said grudgingly, and wondered why her heart was racing so—almost as if she were indeed guilty of the offense.

Sir Basil was still shaking his head in confusion as he saddled Greybeard and rode away. Susannah, for one, would have been surprised indeed to notice his destination that day. Had she ridden out but an hour later, she would have come upon her father deep in conversation with the pariah himself. Sir Basil could have explained it easily—he was often in the habit of visiting one or another of his tenants, and while he was eager to keep his daughter away from MacDougal, for reasons that were obvious to any parent of a beautiful young lady, he himself liked the man.

Perhaps it would have been harder for him to explain why on this particular day their friendly master-tenant conversation appeared to turn into a heated argument. But no one saw them together—with the possible exception of Trunkett, who had a nasty habit of being in two places at one time, as Susannah had often noticed.

Despite her professed speed, Mrs. Maggins had delivered none of the new dresses she was making for the misses Grainly by the time Lord Westbridge took his leave of them before returning to London for the rest of June. He could find no excuse to refuse this dinner invitation on his last day in the country, but he did take the precaution of ingesting a dose of digestive powder before he set out for Birchwood Hall that evening.

As Susannah dressed for dinner, she thought longingly of the white satin gown Mrs. Maggins was making for her when she once again donned the same old yellow frock she had worn at their last dinner party. At least Trunkett had replaced the soiled panel with some material from the original garment; however, the repair was glaring, for it did not match the rest of the gown, which had faded from more frequent wear. Susannah did not really care. Perhaps if Lord Westbridge recalled her dowdiness when he was in town, he would fix his affections on a more suitably dressed female and she would be free of this wretched engagement through no fault of her own.

Lord Westbridge entertained no such dishonorable notions when he greeted his fiancée that evening. He was looking very fine himself. By now his injuries had faded so much that only a slight discoloration beneath both his eyes left any reminder of his former disfigurement, that and the faintest suggestion of a flaw in the patrician sweep of his nose. He was dressed conservatively but elegantly in a dark-blue coat with matching trousers, and his cravat was a snowy-white model of perfection. Looking at him quite dispassionately, Susannah could allow that he was a handsome man, although she had her suspicions that the impressive breadth of his shoulders owed much to the skill of his tailor and little to nature.

"You seem pale tonight, my dear," he remarked to her as they stood together in the drawing room, awaiting the summons to dine.

Susannah felt an unaccountable urge to apologize for this defect, for she did not know whether the remark had been made as a reproach or an expression of concern. "I have been much indoors of late, my lord." She still could not bring herself to call him Ivor without choking a bit on the name, especially in company.

"Susannah has been making much progress on the harpsichord," Lady Grainly declared. "If you would enjoy it, perhaps we could prevail upon her to play for you after dinner."

Susannah's heart sank; she was willing to be much more honest about her talent.

"No, mamma," Lucy protested gently, "we must perform the duet we have been practicing for his lordship, and Susannah does not know how to play that."

Susannah cast her aunt a grateful glance as Lady Grainly gave a grudging approval to this proposal.

Westbridge seemed to enjoy his meal, although the joint was mutton again. Susannah suspected it was part of the same sheep they had served him before, for mutton had not been seen at the Grainly table during the intervening time. However, there was some very nice chicken in a wine sauce and a savory of toasted cheese, so Westbridge finished his dinner with high hopes for his digestion.

The men did not linger long over their port, as Westbridge declared himself anxious to hear the young ladies' performance. This was a lilting country air rendered quite sweetly by Susannah's soprano and Lucy's contralto voices. When it was finished, Westbridge applauded politely, and even Lady Grainly gave a nod of approval. Lucy lingered at the harpsichord, to provide some background music, while Lady Grainly pointedly pulled Sir Basil aside to speak of housekeeping matters, thus leaving Susannah and Westbridge free to hold their own tête-à-tête.

"Your voice is very lovely," he said pleasantly. "I hope I will hear much of it in the future."

"Thank you, my lord," Susannah said, her eyes downcast. She settled herself upon the settee, and Westbridge joined her there.

"Come, come," he said kindly. "There is no reason for you to mope. I will be returning to Westham Park in little more than two weeks' time, and then we will have the whole summer together." He had finally decided that her lowered spirits were caused by sorrow over his imminent departure.

"I will look forward to that," Susannah murmured appropriately.

"Of course, we will be spending a quiet summer, on

account of my stepmother's condition," he warned her. "Still, I don't see why that should prevent us from enjoying a picnic or a drive—and, of course, there will be the fête at the end of July."

"That will be lovely," Susannah said. She tried to picture Westbridge lolling on the grass, enjoying a picnic, but her imagination failed her.

Lady Grainly approached them to say, "I hope you will excuse Basil and me for a moment, Lord Westbridge. We must look up something in the ledger. I am sure Susannah will be happy to entertain you until we have returned." She led Sir Basil out of the door, full of admiration for her own kindness in allowing them to have this private time together for some tender parting words.

Now their only chaperone was Lucy, who was playing upon the harpsichord at the other end of the room. The loudness of the instrument insured that they would not be overheard.

Westbridge sidled a little closer to Susannah and took her hand in his. She felt a sudden urge to withdraw it immediately and run for her bedchamber, but valiantly overcame this rude impulse. Instead, she attempted a tentative smile.

He glanced over at Lucy, who was paying them no attention at all, and then, with no further warning, leaned over and gave Susannah a brief salute upon her lips.

Susannah was too surprised by this to respond in any way, even if she had wished to. Her first thought was that her aunt had been much too enthusiastic when she described a kiss as nice and pleasant, although, under the circumstances, Susannah was more than content to accept the adjectives "brief" and "savorless."

Inadvertently, she glanced toward Lucy, to see if she

had noticed anything of this, and Westbridge smiled indulgently at what he thought was her consideration for convention.

"My dear Susannah," he said softly, retaining his grip on her hand but making no move to take any further liberties, "you have no idea what a breath of fresh air you are to one as town-weary as I have become."

Their new intimacy had reduced Susannah's reserve a little, and she was prompted to voice the first original remark she had ever uttered to Westbridge. "If that is the case, my lord, one is tempted to wonder at your eagerness to return to town."

"Do not be reproachful, Susannah," he chided. "It does not become you."

She flushed slightly and attempted to slide her hand out from under his, but this was impossible, as his palm had become slightly sweaty during this prolonged contact with hers.

"I was not reproaching you, my l—— *Ivor*," she said. "I was merely wondering. I have never been to London, as you well know, and am naturally curious about what attractions it may hold."

"Little enough, if one does not enjoy dancing or theatrical entertainments or making constant chatter with the same people day after day."

"Oh, but I *do* enjoy those things," Susannah said, becoming bolder. "At least I know I like to dance and think I should enjoy the theatre, although my only experience of the latter has not been very wide. I did see the pantomime at Christmastime and was quite enthralled."

"Then I promise I will take you to London next spring," Westbridge said indulgently. "That is, if you are still fit by then."

Susannah was about to ask him why she should not be fit for a visit to town until his meaning struck her and she blushed.

"Your delicacy becomes you, my dear," he said approvingly, "and you must forgive me if I appear too hasty in my desire to start a family. But it is as well that you know the matter of the succession weighs heavy upon my shoulders."

Susannah thought this an odd analogy and wondered if her suspicions on how families were started were even faultier than she knew them to be. "I quite understand, Ivor," she said, then, one thought leading to another, her mind naturally wandered to his reason for haste in this regard and she felt they had progressed far enough that she might quiz him on this delicate subject.

"Is it true that your brother sold government secrets to the French?" she asked him eagerly.

He frowned slightly. "That is something I do not wish to discuss, now or ever," he said flatly.

"But surely, now that I am to be a Westham I should know all about it," Susannah persisted. "What if someone should question me on the subject?"

"Then you will be able to say, quite truthfully, that you know nothing at all about it," he said severely, finally withdrawing his hand from hers.

"I think it is too bad of you not to let me know," Susannah told him. "I promise I wouldn't tell anyone."

"You must allow me to be the judge of what is fit for your ears, my dear. Indeed, I am glad that this subject has arisen, for I can set the example of how I mean to go on. As my wife, Susannah, you must learn to be guided by me in all things." His tone had become quite pedantic as he laid down this law.

"That is rather a sweeping statement," Susannah pointed out playfully. "What exactly do you mean by 'all things'? Are you proposing to extend that even to personal matters, such as when I should have my bath or what I should eat for breakfast?"

"Certainly," Westbridge said, "if I find some fault in the way you perform these functions now."

With dawning horror she realized that he was indeed earnest. "Why, that is the most ridiculous thing I have heard in all my life," she declared, rising and moving away from him. "And what if I do not wish to have my bathtime so regulated?"

"Susannah, I am surprised to find this streak of self-will in you," he said, rising too.

"And I am surprised to find this streak of tyranny in you!" she retorted.

Lucy had paused in her playing at the first sounds of their upraised voices and was now watching the scene in an agony of embarrassment.

"You really must learn to control your temper, Susannah," Westbridge said, looking down at her from his vastly superior height. "I had not been warned that you possessed one."

"And I had not been warned that you fancied yourself to be Zeus himself. Why do you not return to Olympus, my lord? You must be mightily weary of us poor mortals, who are all so stupid we do not even know when we should have a bath!"

"Susannah, control yourself! There is no need to shout. I am standing right in front of you."

"I can easily remedy *that*, my lord." With that remark she turned on her heel and departed, slamming the door as she went. Westbridge was left standing in the middle of the room, fuming and amazed.

"You must forgive my niece," Lucy said, coming to stand beside him. "Remember her youth and make allowances accordingly."

"Of course," Ivor said. "I must apologize for my behavior as well. I forgot myself."

"Not at all," Lucy said. "It is Susannah—she has been out of sorts lately."

"I am sorry to hear it, but now that you have mentioned it, I did notice that she was looking rather pale tonight. I should have been more gentle with her." Then, with a sudden look of concern on his face, "But she is not sickening for something, is she?" He hoped he had not caught something from the little kiss he had bestowed on her.

"You are most generous to be worried about her, but I am certain she will be quite all right," Lucy assured him. "It is just that she has been indoors much of late and has not had a chance to ride as often as she was used to."

"I did not know she was a horsewoman."

"Call her instead a ponywoman," Lucy said with a smile. Then, seeing his look of confusion, she explained, "She does not have a proper horse, only a little pony she loves dearly."

"I did not know, or I certainly would have invited her to ride with me this past week. We have horses to spare at Westham." His stern features softened somewhat. "Despite what she may have said, I am no tyrant. I am more than willing to afford her any little pleasure she might enjoy."

"There is no need to assure *me* of that, Ivor," Lucy said softly. "I have always been aware of your nature."

"My dear Lucy," he said, taking her hand in a friendly

fashion. "I am certain that with your gentle example to follow Susannah will soon be cured of any little quirk of temper she may have."

Lucy flushed pleasurably at this praise. "Thank you, Ivor," she said simply.

❧ CHAPTER SEVEN ❧

ONCE AGAIN SUSANNAH sought the privacy of her own bedchamber when she left Westbridge's side. Once again she flung herself upon the bed, but this time it was with anger, not despair, and she did not weep. She merely pummeled the pillow a few times, pretending it was Westbridge's head as he told her, in that odiously condescending manner of his, that he would consider it his duty to tell her when to bathe. For Susannah it would not be a duty but a pleasure to tell *him* to soak at least one part of his body—the part that housed all those restrictive notions he spouted with such ease. And if he spoke thus while they were engaged, a time when one is generally on one's best behavior, whatever would he be like when they were married? Susannah's fists clenched convulsively as she longed desperately for some way to get out of this hateful engagement, some other way to find the money that would insure her future and the fate of the others at Birchwood Hall.

She heard the soft knock on her door but did not bother to reply, knowing that Lucy would come in whether she willed or not. And so Lucy did, pausing uncertainly in the doorway until she noticed Susannah on the bed, her head buried unsociably under a pillow.

Lucy closed the door softly behind her and perched upon the edge of the bed. Finally, she reached out a tentative hand to touch Susannah on the arm.

"Don't touch me," came a muffled cry from beneath the pillow.

Lucy sighed and withdrew her hand. "Susannah, you are behaving like a child."

"I don't care," Susannah said, then lifted her face and regarded her aunt with a dismal expression. "He kissed me, Aunt Lu, and I don't care what you told me before. It wasn't nice in the least."

Lucy flushed. "Really, Susannah, you should not speak of such things. It was wrong of me to have discussed it with you in the first place." She stood up and moved away from the bed.

"You were right there when he did it," Susannah pointed out, sitting up and arranging her dress, which had become very rumpled. "What was to prevent you from looking up whenever you pleased and catching him in the very act of forcing his attentions on me?"

"Discretion," Lucy said dryly.

"The point is, you lied to me, Aunt Lu," she said with some reproach. "You told me kissing was nice and pleasant, and it was neither of those things. Indeed, it gives me a cold shiver to think about it. Had he not been so quick, I should have avoided his embrace entirely."

"Susannah, he is engaged to you," Lucy said, having turned every shade of red from pink to a deep scarlet. "He has every right to offer you his attentions."

"Well, I don't like it," Susannah declared, very childishly indeed.

"Such things are best left private between you and Ivor. I am sure he would agree with me."

"Oh, yes, your Ivor is a stickler for proprieties. That is why he was so anxious to berate me in front of you at the top of his lungs," Susannah said with wonderful sarcasm.

"If anyone was shouting, it was you," Lucy pointed out.

"And you should know! You had a ringside seat!"

"A ringside seat? I declare I do not know where you pick up such low expressions, Susannah." She regained her self-composure with an effort and said to her niece, "But that is not what I have come in here to discuss. The point is that you have behaved very rudely to Ivor on two occasions—at least two occasions that *I* am aware of. Goodness knows what has taken place between you when you have been alone with him."

"I have never been alone with him," Susannah said, adding, "and I wish I never shall be," in a muttered aside.

"Very well," Lucy conceded, "you have been extremely rude to him on two occasions, and both times I have smoothed things over after you have left."

"Do you know you looked exactly like grandmamma as you said that?" Susannah remarked thoughtfully. "I almost expected to see a walking stick in your hand."

Lucy showed an unexpected flash of temper. "You are not listening to me, Susannah! Were I a telltale I should go straight to mamma and give her a report of what happened tonight and let *her* deal with you, instead of trying to talk sense into you myself.''

Susannah shrugged indifferently. "I am sure she has already heard of it from Trunkett, who is always listening at doors and spying. Why, I shouldn't be at all surprised if she weren't listening to us at this very moment." She crept to the door and flung it open dramatically, almost convinced by now that she would find that redoubtable personage lurking there. But the hallway was empty, and as Susannah closed the door again, disappointed, she caught Lucy's eye and they couldn't help laughing together.

"Aunt Lu, forgive me," Susannah said at last, "but can you not see for yourself what an evil influence Westbridge is? You and I have never argued."

"He is not evil, Susannah," Lucy said quietly. "Ivor is a kind and upright gentleman with a noble nature, and despite what you may think he *does* care for you. He was most anxious about your health tonight and commented that you were looking pale."

Susannah was about to retort sarcastically again, but something in Lucy's tone stopped her. It was quite amazing, but when Lucy spoke about Westbridge her face softened and her eyes grew bright; why, even her figure seemed to improve as she brought her chin up and put her shoulders back, as if something of Westbridge's noble bearing were reflected in her. But once she had observed this phenomenon, Susannah was surprised that she had not noticed it before—it was always thus when Lucy spoke about Westbridge, and even more obvious when she was in his very presence.

"Do you think he will make a good husband, Aunt Lu?" she asked, watching her aunt carefully.

"I cannot think of any man who would make a better." Lucy's voice had the ring of conviction.

"And what of his notions about guiding me in everything? You do not think I should find him too oppressive?"

"I think you should count your blessings that you are to be guided by a man with such a fine sense of honor, who would never allow himself to be led by his baser emotions, but only by what is true and good."

Susannah had never heard her aunt wax so eloquent, and inadvertently she smiled.

"There!" Lucy said with satisfaction, "I knew I could bring you around." She gave her niece an affectionate hug. "I'll wager, too, that you will miss him terribly while he is in London and be very glad to have him back here with us."

"I am sure one of us will miss him," Susannah murmured.

"Pardon? I did not hear what you said, darling."

"Nothing, Aunt Lu. You are quite right. I *have* behaved childishly, but now I see that it will be all right."

After a few more tender words, Lucy left her niece, convinced that she had preserved Ivor's happiness and tranquility, both of which were dearer to her than her own.

Susannah, too, was thinking of Westbridge's happiness, although what she was now planning would not promise tranquility, at least not in the near future. It had become patently obvious to her that Westbridge was marrying the wrong Miss Grainly; somehow things must be contrived so that he should marry the right one. How this would be accomplished was a matter for future speculation and conniving; in the meantime, Susannah was quite content to contemplate her now rosy future. Lucy would marry Westbridge, thereby rescuing the Hall from its dire financial straits, pleasing Lady Grainly, who had long ago written off her daughter as a hopeless spinster, and leaving Susannah free to do as she pleased.

And what exactly did she please to do? Unbidden, her hand reached into her pocket, as it was wont to do at the most inconvenient moments, and pulled out a large, square handkerchief. Even careful laundering had not completely removed the faint, delicious smell of tobacco from it, a smell Susannah could best enjoy if she held the handkerchief against her cheek.

Apparently, Lucy's soothing words had convinced Westbridge to overlook Susannah's fit of pique the night before, for he sent his fiancée a conciliatory note before he left for London that morning. Susannah read this note at the breakfast table, under the eyes of her father and aunt. Had she been alone, she certainly would have torn it in two upon reading Westbridge's fervent hopes for her speedy return to health and good spirits—a thinly disguised warning that she should improve her temper. Susannah tossed the note aside with a sniff.

"Well?" Lucy asked at last, propriety preventing her from satisfying her curiosity as to the contents of the missive by simply taking it up and reading it.

Susannah shrugged indifferently. "He is concerned about my health and says he has prepared a surprise for me that he hopes will soon restore me to my usual good spirits."

"How very thoughtful," Sir Basil said, beaming. "I am so glad to see that you are getting on so well with him." Relieved was actually an apter description of his state of mind; he still hardly dared to hope that he had contracted a happy marriage for his daughter.

"What sort of surprise is it?" Lucy asked.

"I have no idea. Read the note for yourself, if you

like," Susannah offered without hesitation, for it contained nothing of a personal nature unless one considered the closing expression—"Yrs. affectionately, Ivor Westham, Marquess of Westbridge, etc."—too intimate for general perusal. "He mentions you in it," Susannah added.

"How kind of him," Lucy said, a faint pinkness tinging her pale cheeks.

"Perhaps you can guess what the surprise is, Aunt Lu. He says it was your idea."

"Oh, I couldn't begin to guess," Lucy said, but her face was not made for dissembling, and as she read the note she gathered a strong suspicion as to what Westbridge's surprise was.

"You *do* know, Aunt Lu!" Susannah exclaimed, evincing some interest at last. "Do tell me! Is it very nice or merely something boring, like a book of poetry?"

"No, it is not poetry," Lucy laughed.

"No, I expect not," Susannah admitted. "Sermons would be more like his style. Come, Aunt Lu—I shall perish if you do not tell me."

Lucy shook her head. "It is something *very* nice, and that is all I will say about it."

"Whisper in my ear, Lucy," Sir Basil begged; he, too, was now caught up in the suspense.

"I certainly would not tell *you*, Basil," Lucy declared. "You would have it all over the county by noon." She handed the note back to Susannah. "You will probably want to save this, Sukey; it is your first correspondence from him."

Susannah took it back and tucked it away, more for Lucy's benefit than her own. "I shall have it out of you yet," she warned.

101

But Lucy remained quite implacable the rest of that day and all of the next. Indeed, she was worn out by Susannah's pestering, which was stifled only in the presence of Lady Grainly, who was convinced herself that the surprise would turn out to be a piece of jewelry and would hear no more speculation. Susannah soon decided that her grandmother was probably right and resolved to think no more about it. In any case, a gift from Westbridge would have to be returned one day if her still-unformulated plan were put into effect, so it was no use wasting time wondering what it would be. Besides, some of the new clothes had finally arrived from Mrs. Maggins, so she soon had other small delights to occupy her mind.

The next morning Susannah came downstairs dressed in her new riding habit, and while she had expected some admiration from her aunt, she had not expected a crow of delight and an enthusiastic, "Oh, I *am* glad you wore that today."

"Why?" Susannah asked with surprise.

"No reason," Lucy said airily. "Only that it does look very well on you."

"Thank you," Susannah said, and took up a plate to help herself to breakfast.

"Basil wants you to join him in the stables as soon as possible," Lucy remarked presently.

"I will go there when I have eaten," Susannah said.

"I think you will be sorry if you wait," Lucy said playfully. "He wants to show you Ivor's surprise."

Susannah was not a slow wit, and it took her less than ten seconds to realize the import of her aunt's words, put down her plate and dash out to the stable.

Her surprise from Westbridge was in the stable yard,

being admired by Sir Basil and Higgins, the groom from Westham who had brought the horse over.

"Oh, papa, she's beautiful!" Susannah exclaimed breathlessly.

"Indeed she is," Sir Basil affirmed. "We haven't had a horse like this in our stable since—well, for a very long time."

It was a beautiful little bay mare, with dainty white hooves and a white forelock. She had come supplied with her own saddle and bridle; Westbridge always had a passion for details. Susannah reached out and stroked her soft nose, hardly daring to believe she was real. The mare gave a little nicker of greeting and Susannah was in love.

"Has she a name?" Susannah asked.

"Eh, we call her Rapunzel, on account of that shock of golden hair," Higgins said, "but I reckon you can call her anything you like."

"No, Rapunzel will do quite nicely," Susannah said with a little laugh. "It is like a fairy tale that she is mine. May I ride her right away, papa?"

"Perhaps just for a little while, around the stable yard, until we see how she goes," Sir Basil replied.

"She is gentle as a lamb. I am sure of it," Susannah said.

"Eh, she's gentle enough," Higgins averred. "A mite skittish now and then, but that's only to be expected of a lady like her." He led the horse over to the mounting block and helped Susannah up.

"Well, what do you think?" Sir Basil asked.

"I certainly have a better view up here than I do on little Bessy," Susannah exclaimed. She put the horse through her paces and found that she had a sensitive mouth and responded beautifully to her mistress's commands.

"She is lovely, papa," Susannah said. "May I not ride her farther off? I am sure she will not shy or run away with me. We understand one another quite well already, don't we, Rapunzel?" She leaned forward and cooed some tender words in the mare's ear, and the horse seemed to nod in agreement.

"Well," Sir Basil said hesitantly, "perhaps if I saddled up Greybeard and accompanied you."

"But papa, Greybeard will never be able to keep up with my beautiful Rapunzel," Susannah protested. "I promise I won't go far. I will take the bridle path through the woods to the Winnow farm and back. That is no distance at all—I will be back in a quarter of an hour."

Sir Basil was reluctant to let her ride off alone on a strange horse so soon, but he had pressing matters to attend to before he began his regular rounds. It was quite true, too, that Greybeard would not be able to keep up with Rapunzel. Then again, Susannah was hard to resist when she pleaded with him so engagingly, and she had so few pleasures. How could he refuse her?

Susannah did not set out to deceive her father; she had every intention of riding only as far as the Winnow farm and returning straightaway, as she had promised. But the cottage on the Lewis farm was only a short distance further; indeed, the lands of the Lewis farm lay to her right as she guided the mare down the path, but she caught sight of no bright red head working there. She did pass George Winnow to the left and waved to him politely, noticing with amusement the extra long stare he gave her as she proceeded in all her new finery.

She reached the point where the path branched off to the right, and although it had only been a few weeks since she had taken that turning, it seemed like a lifetime ago. She wondered what harm there would be in taking it one last time, perhaps to prove to herself that she had indeed outgrown her childish infatuation and would no longer succumb to the dubious charms of the Scotsman. She had little doubt that MacDougal would reveal himself to be the ill-educated brute she had described to her father; after two weeks of daily intercourse with the handsome Lord Westbridge and his impeccable manners, elegant dress, and learned discourse, she had a new awareness of what a gentleman should be and would probably laugh at herself for ever suspecting that Sandy MacDougal was among their number.

As she rode the few dozen rods to the Lewis cottage she practiced the cold, ladylike nod she would give the tenant, how she would politely—but condescendingly—ask after his health and the progress of his crops. Perhaps she would even return his handkerchief, handing it back to him with a whimsical—but distant—smile, indicating clearly that she appreciated his former kindness but knew they both understood that all such associations were now at an end.

At last she saw him, kneeling in his kitchen garden in his shirtsleeves—so common!—pulling weeds and consulting that ever-present volume of poetry.

Susannah's heart gave a sickening little lurch when she saw this, and had she not known better, she would have thought it was caused by jealousy. How ridiculous to be jealous of some Scottish lassie who obviously knew what she was about to send this fellow packing!

"Good day to you, MacDougal," Susannah said as coldly as she could.

He looked up with surprise, for he had not heard her approach, being engrossed in his work. "Guid day t'ye, miss," he said, rising and dusting himself off. He reached for his tweed coat, which was hanging on a convenient post, and quickly put it on, tucking the book away in the inside pocket, so as to be in more suitable attire to address his master's daughter.

"Tis a verra fine horse ye hae, miss," he said politely.

Susannah had forgotten how thick his accent was; she supposed she had grown used to it before. "Thank you, MacDougal," she said. "It was a gift from my fiancé, Lord Westbridge."

"She looks t' be a fine gaer, miss," Sandy said.

"Naturally, all of the Westham horses are of racing stock." Susannah's nose was tingling from her efforts to speak through it. "And how is your garden faring, MacDougal?"

"Verra weel, miss, thank ye," he replied. His tone was respectful enough, but was that laughter she saw behind his eyes?

She moved a little closer to him so that he could experience the full magnificence of her new finery and know what a vast social gap existed between them. She examined his garden as she thought her father might when he was looking after the tenants to see how they were progressing.

"Excuse me, MacDougal, but may I ask why you are pulling up all your carrots so soon?" she asked suddenly when she was close enough to see what he had been busy at. Her surprise that he should be systematically destroying the garden he had spent so many hours tending made her forget to speak through her nose.

"I'm pullin' the weeds, miss," he said, and looked uncertainly at the handful of greenery he held.

"But those are carrots you are pulling up, not weeds," Susannah pointed out.

" 'Tis better for the ones left if ye pull oot some o' the others thae are a wee bit sma'," he said decidedly.

"Quite true, but you must leave *some* to grow." Susannah was about to laugh, but then remembered he had been weeding with the book of poetry open before him. Obviously, he had been so lost in thoughts of his erstwhile lover that he had not paid proper attention to the matter at hand. "Perhaps I should speak to my father," she suggested, imperious again. "He would not care to know that one of his tenants was mismanaging his land in such a fashion."

Sandy regarded her curiously. The threat did not worry him—Sir Basil was not a man to evict one of his tenants for pulling up a few carrots by mistake, but something in the overly proud lift of Susannah's head made him decide to play along.

"Nae, miss, ye wudna do thae t' puir me," he whined, enjoying himself immensely. "Tis nae mair than a puir wee bit o' carrot. If I was t' be turned off my land, the Guid Laird ken weel whae wud becoo o' me. Please, miss, I beg ye, ye maunna tell the maister."

Susannah was surprised at first, then her sense of humor got the best of her. "Sandy, you are doing it much too brown!" she laughed. "I beg you to stop!"

"Nae, miss, tis only thae ye put the fear o' God in my puir peasant heart," he said.

"Nonsense, I did nothing of the kind," she laughed, and in a moment he was laughing with her.

"Thae's better, miss. Now ye look t' be yer former sell agin. Troth, I dinna ken ye at the first."

Shyly, Susannah asked, "Do you like my new clothes, Sandy?"

"Aye," he replied, "they're verra fine. Ye hae becoo quite the young leddy, miss, and shudna be idlin' wi' the likes o' me. Indaid, yer own father hae warned me agin speakin' t' ye.''

"As he has warned me against you," Susannah said.

"Weel, then, miss, we hae naught mair t' say t' one another. If ye'll be excusin' me, I'll get back t' my weedin'." He turned his back on her abruptly and pulled up a few more carrots.

"Very well, MacDougal," Susannah said severely, hurt by this sudden dismissal but successfully keeping a catch out of her voice. She pulled the mare around sharply—a little too sharply, for Rapunzel had been growing restive, and the unexpected force on her delicate mouth, combined with the sight of a large rabbit in front of her, made her shy and rear slightly. Susannah fell off.

Sandy ran up to her immediately and knelt down beside her to help her to her feet. "Lassie! Are you all right?" The concern on his face struck her forcibly, and his strong arms helping her to her feet felt so warm and comfortable that she was reluctant to be released from them.

"I think I have twisted my ankle," she said, sinking down again.

"Which one?"

"The right one," Susannah decided.

In a moment he was examining the injured area delicately, asking Susannah if it hurt *there* or *there*.

"Oh, yes, terribly," Susannah said, heroically keeping a smile of pleasure from her face.

"Do you think if I lifted you onto your horse you would be able t' ride back t' the Hall?" he asked. The mare had strayed only a few yards and was now contentedly munching on carrot greens, indifferent to the scene being played out nearby. "I'll lead your horse, o' course," he added, "and make certain you arrive back safely."

Susannah did not miss the fact that the burr had almost completely disappeared from his voice, but had no leisure to reflect upon it now.

"Perhaps if I put my arms around your neck," she suggested, and he moved closer to comply with this request, placing his arms about her waist at the same time and thus managing to lift them both to a standing position.

Sandy was not a very tall man, but he was just the right height for Susannah, and her head fit comfortably against his shoulder once they were upright.

"Do you think you can make it over t' your horse?" he asked, "or would you like me t' carry you?"

"If you help me, perhaps I can hobble over," she said, enjoying the smell of tobacco and the prickly-smooth feel of his coat against her cheek.

"Are you quite sure you are all right?" he asked. "You seem flushed."

"Do I?" she asked, looking up into his face. "But then, so do you."

The temptation was too great, and Sandy was only a man, after all, not a stick of wood who could not be moved by such close proximity to a lady as beautiful as Susannah. He drew her closer and kissed her, and in the heat of the moment did not notice that she was planted firmly on two feet to meet his embrace.

It was nothing like the kiss she had received from Lord Westbridge, Susannah realized with delight. She had wronged her aunt by calling her a liar, but then Lucy had not been effusive enough in her description. It was far more than just nice, or even pleasant—it was glorious, exciting, wonderful—Susannah was no longer interested in describing the experience, but only in enjoying it.

She did not know how long they remained thus. While it

was happening the kiss seemed to last an eternity, but it was too soon when he released her.

"Forgi'e me, miss," he said roughly, withdrawing from her.

"There is nothing to forgive," Susannah said, her eyes shining.

"Ye haena hurt yersell at all," he said accusingly.

"Yes, I have," she protested. "It comes and goes—like your accent."

He couldn't help grinning, for he had been fairly caught out. "And to imagine that I thought you a wee bairn of thirteen and no more."

"Sometimes I wish I were, for then we should at least be friends again. I have missed you, Sandy."

"And I have missed you, Susannah." It was the first time he had ever used her name; previously it had always been "lassie" or "miss." He liked the sound of it.

"Can we not be friends again?" she asked softly.

He had to struggle against the impulse to embrace her once more. "Ye ha best be gettin' hame, miss," he said, slipping back into the thick accent as if it were a refuge. "Before yer fine new horse eats a' the carrots I haena pulled up myself."

He took her gently but firmly by the arm, led her to the horse, and helped her up. The air seemed thick between them with words unsaid, but while Susannah longed to tell him what was in her heart, she could not muster the courage to do so. He seemed to want to tell her something, too; indeed, several times he took in breath as if to speak, only to exhale it again, unused.

So rapt were they both in their thoughts that they did not hear the steady clop-clop of approaching hooves until Sir Basil was upon them.

"So this is how you use my trust!" he exclaimed. "To sneak off behind my back!"

"Papa!" Susannah cried. "I was just passing by. Rapunzel shied and threw me and Sandy helped me back on." But even though she spoke much that was true, the words sounded like a lie.

"'Tis just as she said, maister," Sandy added unconvincingly.

"Susannah, I have told you that you are to have nothing to do with this man. If I discover that you have gone against me again, I will have no choice but to turn him off the estate."

"Oh, no, papa! Please don't do that! It wasn't Sandy's fault."

Sir Basil's anger seemed out of proportion to the simple crime of passing the time of day with a tenant. Susannah wondered if he might have seen something more, but surely this was not possible else he would have made his presence known sooner.

"As for you, MacDougal," Sir Basil went on, "keep away from my daughter. This is not the first time I have told you this, but by God it will be the last."

"Yes, sir," Sandy replied respectfully.

Susannah wondered why he made no protest, no effort to defend himself, until she realized that he was indeed guilty of what Sir Basil had warned her about—he had taken liberties with her! But it wasn't his fault! she wished to cry out. She had engineered the entire thing, had pretended she was hurt.

"Your grandmother will be very disappointed in you, Susannah," Sir Basil said sternly. "As indeed I am myself. I came after you only because you were gone longer than I had expected and I thought you might be in some difficulty.

Little did I think you had taken advantage of this opportunity to go against my express wishes. I see now that you are not to be trusted, and I am disappointed.''

''Yes, papa,'' Susannah said, hanging her head. Indeed, he was quite right—she was *not* to be trusted. If she thought she could get away with it, she would come visit Sandy as often as possible, but this she could not do. Her carelessness had already brought him close to eviction. He would be no more than wise if he never spoke to her again for fear of invoking his master's further wrath and losing his very livelihood. Susannah must avoid him at all costs to keep them both away from temptation.

Why did her father hate Sandy so?

⊶(CHAPTER EIGHT)⊷

SUSANNAH FOLLOWED HER father back to Birchwood Hall, but he spoke not another word to her except when they were grooming the horses and then only to remark, as if to himself, that he would have to get a lad in to see to the stable, for with the new horse he could not do it all himself.

She waited nervously the rest of the day for the lecture she would receive from her grandmother about her disobedience, but this never came. Evidently, Sir Basil thought the strain on his mother's heart would be too great. Susannah knew, too, that Trunkett had been shopping in the village that morning so could not have been spying on *her*—and the only other person who had seen her riding toward the Lewis farm was George Winnow, a taciturn man who minded his own business.

Several days later a new addition was made to the

Birchwood Hall staff in the form of young Will Tucker, who was to look after the stables and accompany Susannah on her rides, usually trailing along far behind on little Bessy, but, as ordered, never letting Miss Grainly out of his sight. Susannah chafed under this new supervision, but there was nothing she could do about it. Much as she wanted to see Sandy again, she could not risk it—the consequences would be too dire. He would be turned off the estate and left without a livelihood, and she would probably be guarded even more closely and left with no opportunity to carry out her yet unformulated plan to bring Lucy and Westbridge together. If she had gained anything from her visit to the Lewis farm it was the unswerving conviction that no power on earth could force her to marry Westbridge—not when she loved another.

A few days later the solicitors arrived from London with copies of the marriage settlement for Sir Basil to sign. Soon there was a new lightness in his step and at mealtimes he was full of plans for the future. He called in contractors and received an estimate for repairs on the Hall's drains, and was in correspondence with a man who would sell him a hundred head of cattle once they could agree on a price. A new herd would mean they would need to have the fences repaired, so Sir Basil called in another set of contractors to estimate that job. His mouth seldom twitched anymore from his nervous tic, and he was even putting on some weight as he contemplated the now rosy future of his beloved lands.

Lady Grainly, too, was in a cheerful mood much of the time and complained less frequently of her arthritis and heart palpitations. In a three-day frenzy of epistolary zeal, she worked her way down her entire list of correspondents, spreading the joyful news of her granddaughter's engagement.

After reading the marriage contract most carefully—employing her eyeglass to examine the more complicated passages—she allowed Cook to run up quite a large bill with the butcher, laying in hams, bacon, and cured beef, and took on a young girl from the village as a parlormaid. Westbridge's bride no longer had to clean up after her own muddy boots. Indeed, Lady Grainly was pleased to note that Susannah was much more careful about things like that lately and hardly ever needed reminders anymore. She decided that Susannah's lessons could be shortened now, as she had much else to occupy her time.

Susannah employed the extra leisure thus afforded her by doing a great deal of reading—mostly novels. Somewhere, somehow, she must come up with an idea, a plan that would serve both to end her engagement and assure Lucy's. The second point was the most critical, for it was vital that the Westham money should come to Birchwood Hall, especially now that so much of it was already being spent. But she failed to find even the seed of an idea that would turn the trick. Ways to break off an engagement were numerous and diverse—she could go into a decline, join a convent, disguise herself as a servant and run off to London, or even join a circus—but in all the novels the lover who was so jilted ended up alone. Indeed, he was usually the villain and came to a bad end altogether, but while Susannah did not care for Westbridge, he was not precisely villainous; he would certainly make someone—preferably Lucy—a good husband. Dismissing all these alternatives one after the other, Susannah decided there was nothing she could do until Westbridge returned to the country, unless she could find an opportunity to approach her father directly. After all, it should not be such a difficult thing to accomplish if he were on her side; an exchange of letters and the substitution of Lucy's name for her own on the marriage contract would do quite nicely. But the right moment for this frank confrontation never seemed to present itself.

Then one morning, when she was entering the drawing room to wait upon her grandmother, she was surprised by the smile of real pleasure with which Lady Grainly greeted her.

"Susannah, I have had the nicest letter from the duchess of Duxton," she said pleasantly. "She is very happy to learn of your engagement and has enclosed a clipping of the announcement from the London paper. Would you like to see it?"

"Of course," Susannah lied, taking the slip of paper from her grandmother.

Ivor Westham, Marquess of Westbridge, Colonel (ret.) of the 9th Cavalry, son of Horace Westham, Duke of Duxton, of Westham Park, Northhamptonshire, and the late Margaret Spenser of Somerset, to marry Miss Susannah Grainly, daughter of Sir Basil Grainly, Baronet, of Birchwood Hall, Northhamptonshire, and the late Frances Wigget of Duxtonbury. Marriage date to be announced.

Susannah stared at the words, trying to make sense of them. For the first time she saw the fact of her engagement written down, in black and white, for all the world to read. She was to marry Ivor Westham, marquess of Westbridge, etc., and no silly plan culled from the pages of a novel would rescue her from her plight.

Her grandmother's voice came to her as if in a dream. ". . . And her grace says that they will be returning to the

116

country on the first of July, and we are all invited to dinner on the second. Thank goodness your evening dresses are ready at last. I, of course, will wear my mulberry satin.''

''Pardon?'' Susannah asked vaguely.

There was a flush of annoyance on her grandmother's face. ''I do wish you would listen when I am speaking to you, Susannah,'' she said. ''I would think you should be glad Lord Westbridge is returning.''

''Oh, yes, of course,'' Susannah said, and in a way she *was* glad, for something *must* happen soon. Indeed, she would speak to her father immediately and if she were able to convince him that Lucy was the better bride for Westbridge, they could confront Westbridge together with the slight alteration in his marriage plans.

''Excuse me, grandmamma,'' she said, ''but I would like to show this to papa.''

''Of course,'' Lady Grainly said graciously; her grand-daughter was indeed in high favor lately, and she was quick to forgive her little lapses as only natural in a young girl contemplating her approaching wedding.

With some trepidation but firm resolve, Susannah approached the door to her father's office, ready to renegotiate her future. She was about to knock forcefully when she heard voices on the other side of the door and realized her father was not alone.

''You're bein' totally unreasonable about this, Grainly,'' a strong voice was insisting.

''Look here, you know my mother's views on the matter. She has a weak heart—I couldn't risk—''

''Good God, man, are you forever t' be under the thumb of your mother? Grow up, or I'll have no further use for you!''

Susannah's eyes widened as she recognized Sandy's

voice and wondered that he could speak to her father in such a way. Sir Basil had already threatened him with eviction; had he now called his tenant in to make good on that threat? And what had her grandmother to do with it? Perhaps Trunkett *had* spied on them that morning—the sneaky little snake—and brought her tale to Sir Basil. Susannah had an urge to rush in to defend Sandy from any false allegations that may have been made against him, but her father's next words stopped her.

"Now, now, Sandy," Sir Basil was saying in a wheedling tone, "you know I could never thank you enough for what you have done for me, but—"

"I'll have no more buts! I've played along with your little game long enough. I'll admit I was enjoyin' myself, but this business has put a different complexion on the matter."

"I don't see why—it was never part of our arrangement."

"Aye, and you took great care t' see that it shouldna be, tellin' me she was no more than thirteen years of age and now forbiddin' me to pay my court in a perfectly respectable manner."

With a start Susannah realized they were arguing about *her*.

"And why should I allow you to pay her court? I have already arranged a suitable marriage for her. Besides that, what makes you think she would have you? Your very name must be hateful to her, and she told me herself she thought you an ill-educated brute."

Sandy's hearty laughter rang out, and Susannah could picture just how he must have thrown his head back to give vent to his amusement.

"I am glad you find it all so amusing," Sir Basil said prissily. "I hope you will excuse me now. We have nothing further to discuss."

"We shall see about that," Sandy said pleasantly. "I'm a patient man, Grainly. This wedding will not take place for many months yet, and much may happen in that time." There was the sound of a chair scraping across the floor. "I'll be takin' my lave o' ye now, maister. But remember —ye may hae stopped me seein' her—the Laird ken ye hae the puir lassie guarded like a felon—but ye canna stop me thinkin' o' her."

"We have nothing further to discuss," Sir Basil said, a little desperately. "And by God, I really *will* have you evicted if you bring up the subject again."

"I live in fear o' yer wrath, maister," Sandy said calmly, and opened the door to find himself staring directly into Susannah's sparkling eyes.

"Good morning, Sandy," she said breathlessly.

"Guid mornin', miss," Sandy said with an elaborate bow. "But ye maunna be talkin' t' the likes o' me. Yer father does na care for it, and yer granddam wud hae a heart attack."

Sir Basil cleared his throat. "You may go now, MacDougal."

"Guid day t' ye, *maister*," Sandy said, but before he left he gave Susannah a large wink and whispered, "Dinna fash yersell, lassie." She almost giggled with delight until she saw her father's thunderous expression.

"Susannah, I thought I told you to have nothing more to do with that man," Sir Basil said sternly.

Susannah entered the room. "But papa, I have not. I was coming to see you. I had no idea you were talking to anyone."

"We were discussing his barley crop," Sir Basil said, and she gave no indication that she disbelieved him. "What did you want to see me about?"

"I don't remember," she said lightly. Sir Basil's mood at the moment did not appear to be one that was open to suggestion, so she quickly abandoned her resolution to speak to him. "It was nothing important." The only thing that was important to her now was the knowledge that Sandy had been working toward the same ends as she, only in a different direction. She wished to go off alone and clutch this knowledge to her bosom, like a lovely gift. Sandy wished to marry her and was willing even to risk his livelihood for her!

It was now more important than ever that she bring Westbridge and Lucy together, and quickly, too. She must be free—free of all obligation and responsibility, free to marry a poor tenant farmer if she chose to.

Mrs. Maggins and her staff of local girls had outdone themselves, Susannah thought with satisfaction as she admired her elegant form in the looking glass. Even though she could not obtain a full view of herself in the tiny glass, what she could see convinced her that garbed as she was, she would not have disgraced the finest drawing room in all of England.

The gown was of white satin with an overskirt of white lace that fluttered and floated gracefully with her every move. The sash was of pink satin, as were her new slippers, which peeped provocatively from beneath the hem of her garment. Trunkett had been spared from Lady Grainly's side long enough to dress Susannah's hair in a more elaborate style than she was used to, and while Susannah had been required to spend the afternoon in curl papers, the result was well worth any discomfort she may have suffered. A few tiny pink rosebuds were tucked in between the curls here and there, to finish off her coiffure.

Susannah was practicing curtseys when a knock came upon her door and Lucy entered.

"Aunt Lu, you look lovely," Susannah exclaimed, and Lucy flushed with pleasure at this compliment. Her dress was of pale blue, the same blue as her eyes, and the ribbon of darker blue that trimmed the neckline emphasized the whiteness of her shoulders and neck. She wore a single sapphire on a pendant, but before Susannah could exclaim over this, Lucy held out a string of pearls.

"Mamma says you are to wear these, Sukey," Lucy said.

"Oh, Aunt Lu, how wonderful!" Susannah cried with delight as she allowed Lucy to fasten the string about her neck. It was the very touch that was needed; the pearls seemed to glow against her white bosom, which had never been revealed quite as much as it was tonight.

"You look beautiful, Sukey," Lucy told her sincerely, and this sentiment was echoed by Lady Grainly when they met in the hallway to await the carriage that was being sent for them from Westham Park.

"But please remember, Susannah," Lady Grainly added, unable to resist any opportunity to instill manners in her granddaughter, "that a lady is no more beautiful than her behavior. So while you may be dressed in the first stare of fashion, if you do not comport yourself as a young lady of breeding ought, all the finery and frippery are for naught."

"Yes, grandmamma," Susannah said, bowing her head obediently.

Lady Grainly was a perfect example of this maxim, for she was certainly not dressed in the first stare of fashion. The gown she wore was twenty years old at least, and its voluminous draperies and stiff underpadding were in sharp contrast to the narrow, floating skirts of the two younger ladies. However, there was no one who could deny she was every inch the great lady; she held herself proudly, with the Grainly diamonds sparkling brightly around her neck.

"Basil!" she thundered presently, "Where are you? I hear the carriage outside and you are not ready!"

"Coming, mamma," Sir Basil answered as he came down the stairway, giving his cravat a final tug.

"You take longer to dress than any female I have ever known," she complained as Simons opened the front door and Sir Basil led them out.

"But then, I did not begin my toilet until you ladies had been at it for hours," Sir Basil said with a twinkle.

"Then you should have started earlier." Lady Grainly had no ear for such pleasantries that bore the faint whiff of an insult. "You know what a strain it is upon my heart to be forced to stand and wait for any period of time."

"Yes, mamma," he said weakly.

In a matter of minutes they were driven the two miles to the doors of Westham Park, where they were welcomed by the duke and duchess and quickly provided with refreshment and comfortable seats.

The duchess giggled as she seated herself heavily in a chair that was well supplied with cushions to support her back. "Ivor is taking such a time dressing tonight," she said with a significant look toward Susannah. "I cannot imagine why." She giggled again. She was scarcely older than Lucy and looked even younger, with her fair hair and large, innocent brown eyes.

"Well, well, my dear Susannah," the duke said in his hearty manner. "You have grown up while our backs were turned. It is lucky for us that Ivor noticed it in time and caught you before some other gentleman snatched you right from under our noses."

Susannah could not help smiling at this pleasantry, although she did not quite agree with it. She had always liked the duke; it was not so long ago that she used to bounce happily upon his knee and search for sweets in his pockets.

"Do you know, Phoebe," the duke continued, addressing his wife, "I had never noticed before how our Susannah resembles you."

All in the party were invited to make the comparison, and indeed the resemblance was quite striking, at least in terms of coloring.

"Of course, we are not at all alike in figure," Phoebe giggled, unselfconsciously patting her thickening waistline.

"We will let Ivor take care of that, shall we?" the duke said with a wink at Susannah that caused her to blush. Fortunately, she was saved from replying by the arrival of two more members of the Westham household.

Lord Fenworth was the duchess's son by her first marriage, a boy of about fourteen who also had the fair hair and brown eyes that Phoebe and Susannah shared. He was accompanied by his tutor, a young man of about eight-and-twenty with a swarthy complexion and dark, curling hair.

"You all remember my stepson, Richard," the duke said. "He, too, has been doing some growing. And this is his tutor, Mr. Smollett."

The young earl was a handsome boy and well spoken, but the same could not be said of his tutor, who smiled rather too much for courtesy and attempted some awkward compliments, which caused Lady Grainly to raise her eyeglass and view him more closely. He made Susannah uncomfortable with his close scrutiny of her person, as he, too, remarked upon her resemblance to the duchess.

"It is a combination I have always admired," he said, showing a great many teeth when he smiled. "There is nothing more alluring than a lady with dark eyes and light hair. I do hope his lordship does not let you slip through his fingers as his last fiancée did, but I think you are much too pretty and charming for him to lose his grasp on *you*." He leaned closer to her and said confidentially, "*You* haven't any young man about who might wish to take a punch at his lordship, eh?" He gave a laugh, or rather a hiss punctuated by a sort of hiccough.

Susannah was offended by his overly familiar manner but did not feel that she could be openly rude to him. He was a member of the duke's household, after all. So she merely smiled warily and said nothing. She was relieved when Westbridge entered a few moments later and glad of the propriety that dictated he should stand by her side. Whatever his faults, at least Ivor did not make her skin crawl as this Smollett person most certainly did.

"You are looking very well, my dear," Westbridge said to her.

"Thank you, Ivor," she replied. His name came out more smoothly now; she had been practicing. "Did you enjoy your stay in London?"

"Certainly, but I am glad to be back, nonetheless," he answered. "Lucy is looking very well tonight, too," he remarked presently after one of the frequent pauses that always marked their conversations together.

"Why don't you tell her so?" Susannah suggested boldly. "It would please her very much." Lucy was not speaking to anyone at the moment, so Susannah beckoned her to her side.

124

"Ivor has something to tell you," she said.

He cleared his throat uncomfortably. "It was nothing—that is, I was merely remarking to Susannah that you looked very fine tonight."

"Thank you," Lucy said, pleased. "I am sure Susannah has been telling you how much she enjoys your gift to her. She is out riding every day."

"Why, no, she has not mentioned it," Ivor said with the smallest hint of reproach. "We must ride together now that I have returned, Susannah."

"Of course," she murmured. "I have been looking forward to that."

There was another pause until Westbridge addressed Lucy once more.

"Will you play for us after dinner, Lucy? I remember how you were always so eager to play upon the pianoforte whenever you came to visit here."

"I would love to," she agreed readily. "I find it a much more versatile instrument than the harpsichord, which always seems to sound the same no matter what is being played."

"I would not know the difference in any case," Ivor said with a small smile. "I profess no knowledge in matters musical. Still, I know it gives you pleasure, Lucy."

Dinner was announced, and Susannah was pleased to allow the two of them to continue their conversation at the table, where she need take no part in it. She was seated between the duke and Lord Fenworth, who were both far more congenial companions, as far as she was concerned. Lord Fenworth instantly endeared himself to her by speaking against Smollett.

"You must not allow yourself to be alone with him," he warned her. "The duke has got him on the cheap for the summer because he was kicked out of his last place. Made advances in the wrong quarters, if you know what I mean.''

"I certainly have no wish to be alone with him, my lord,'' Susannah said with a shudder.

"Oh, please call me Richard, and I shall call you Susannah,'' he said cheerfully, "and we will deal together splendidly.'' His voice was once again colored with foreboding. "Of course, the duke figures he cannot get into any trouble here, since mamma's in a *certain condition*, but I wouldn't trust him as far as I could throw him. Although I probably could throw him pretty far,'' he added reflectively.

"Surely the duke should not have employed him if he has a bad reputation,'' Susannah suggested.

"Oh, he's funny about things like that. Always likes to save a penny where he can, even though he's rolling in money. And it is only for the summer, after all. I will be going back to school in the autumn.''

"It seems a strange way to economize—employing a man such as *that*,'' Susannah said.

"That's the duke's way,'' Richard said with a shrug, helping himself to a large serving of stuffed partridge. "Although you would think the duke had learned his lesson long ago. After all, it was his penny-pinching ways that got Ingram into trouble.'' He whispered the name, for it was not a welcome one at this table.

"Oh, do tell me about that! I am simply longing to know,'' Susannah begged him, her eyes shining with anticipation.

He shook his head slightly, casting a nervous glance about. "Not here,'' he said, "but I will tell you some time, if you like. Remind me to do so.''

"I certainly shall,'' Susannah said decidedly.

They chatted on about other things as they ate their dinner. Richard told her about his own home, which he had not seen in some years, because it was let out until he reached his majority.

"My uncle takes care of all that for me," he told her, "that is, my father's brother. I expect I will find that I am rolling in money, too, someday."

"Don't you miss your home?" Susannah asked. "I should be desolate if I had to leave Birchwood for so long a time."

Richard shrugged again and speared a potato. "I don't mind," he said when he had consumed this morsel. "I like spending my summers here, on account of the fête. There's one place where the duke don't spare the brass—and a good thing, too."

"Yes, I enjoy the fête myself," Susannah agreed enthusiastically. "I especially like to have my fortune told by the gypsies, although grandmamma doesn't really approve of it. Will they be here again this summer?"

"I expect so," Richard said. "They make a lot of money out of it, you know. But Susannah, you really should not take what they say too seriously," he warned her.

"Of course not," Susannah agreed cheerfully. "Last year, they told me that I would marry happily and never wander far from the house of my childhood and have lots of children. It sounds like the sort of thing they could tell anyone with a reasonable expectation of its coming true."

"But you *are* going to marry my stepbrother," Richard pointed out, "and Westham Park is not so very far from the home of your childhood, so perhaps there is something in it after all."

"Perhaps," Susannah agreed, thinking of another alternative that would let her live on the very grounds of Birchwood. "Of course, I still think they tell all the girls the same thing. What sort of thing do they tell boys?"

"That I will do well in my studies in spite of obstacles," he said around a piece of roast beef.

"Oh dear, do you suppose they meant Mr. Smollett?" Susannah said with a suppressed giggle.

"I am quite certain they did," Richard laughed. "I have never met anyone who more closely resembles an obstacle." They both laughed together and were unaware of Lord Westbridge's disapproving glance across the table. "My stepbrother does not approve of the gypsies, you know," Richard continued. "I hope that when you are duchess you will be able to convince him that he is wrong. It is quite true that they purloin a number of chickens each year, and occasionally even a sheep, but the duke has always winked his eye at that sort of thing, for they more than earn their keep in entertainment value alone. Did you see the juggler last year? *Much* more exciting than the fortune teller. He juggled with torches of real flame!"

"I missed that," Susannah said with a regretful sigh. "Grandmamma always makes us come away so early— she does not approve of such things either."

"Then you must make a point of waiting this time," Richard told her decidedly. "The juggler is one of the highlights of the fête, as far as I am concerned."

"Are you two talking about my fête?" the duke asked, overhearing the last of their conversation when he turned away from Lady Grainly, who sat on his right. "It is going to be quite something this year," he said proudly. "Do not spread this around, but I think there is a possibility that I can have the pantomime come and play for us. They will be in the county that week, so it might be arranged." He went on to describe the other delights he was planning and promised Susannah earnestly that it would be the best fête ever held in Duxtonbury. He was still talking about it when Phoebe rose and indicated that it was time for the ladies to withdraw.

"He does go on and on about that fête," she giggled to Susannah as they returned to the drawing room. "I have heard it all a hundred times, but I still must pretend I am terribly interested." She sank back onto her comfortable chair and invited Susannah to sit nearby. "We have much to discuss if you are going to come and live with us soon. Have you set any date for the wedding?"

"Not yet, your grace," Susannah said.

"We had thought a New Year's wedding would be convenient," Lady Grainly put in. "Considering your grace's condition, we could not have it much before then."

Phoebe giggled at this reference to her approaching confinement. "Then that gives us plenty of time to make plans," she said. "And in the meantime, I hope you will not be strangers here. I shan't be able to get out much myself, but I do like company."

"I myself would be pleased to call upon you, your grace," Lady Grainly said, "but my ill health would necessarily make those calls infrequent. However, I am certain both Susannah and Lucy will be pleased to avail themselves of your invitation." Both young ladies agreed that this would be so.

"Splendid!" Phoebe said. "Then you must begin by coming to tea tomorrow. All the men are going to the races, and I shall be left quite alone. It will give us a chance to make plans for some redecorating, Susannah."

It was not redecorating that Susannah wished to plan for, but she promised the duchess that she and Lucy would arrive shortly after noon to bear her company.

~❦《 CHAPTER NINE 》❦~

SUSANNAH AND LUCY'S visit to Westham Park was more informal than the dinner party had been the night before. The duchess entertained them in the morning room, and they were introduced to her two younger sons, lords Jasper and Leslie, who were displayed proudly by their nurse. Lord Leslie was only just beginning to walk, and his mother watched him fondly as he tottered a few steps then fell down with a thump and a look of surprise.

"I am hoping for a girl this time," Phoebe confided in them. "Boys are all very well and good, but they grow up too quickly. My little Dickie has become quite a young man already and does not play with me anymore as he used."

Her two visitors murmured sympathetically. At length, Lord Leslie was pronounced ready for his nap, and the two little boys were taken away.

"Now, Susannah, I should like to show you the rooms that will be yours when you come to live with us," Phoebe said. "They are in a dreadful state, and I am quite determined to have them completely redone. Naturally, I will welcome your opinions on the matter. Yours, too, Lucy," she added graciously.

"If you don't mind, your grace, I would much rather stay behind and play upon the piano," Lucy said. "It is not often that I have an opportunity to do so by myself."

Susannah tried to hide her delight at this suggestion; she longed to speak to the duchess alone. After an almost sleepless night, she had decided that she would try to enlist Phoebe as an ally in her cause, but did not know how she could broach the subject with Lucy always hanging about.

"Why, then, you must come and play whenever you like," Phoebe told Lucy. "No one here uses the instrument much—the first duchess was the only musician in the family, and Lady Imogen, too, I believe, but she is not often here." She made sure that Lucy was comfortably settled and showed her where the first duchess kept her music sheets, before leading Susannah upstairs to the suite of rooms she would share with Westbridge when they were married.

"As you see, it is all quite dismal," she said with an apologetic giggle. "Ivor still uses the room that was his as a child, so no one has lived here since Horace brought his first bride home. Oh dear, just look at these draperies! It is too embarrassing." She shook out one of the window draperies, and a great cloud of dust flew up.

When they had both finished coughing and laughing, Susannah remarked, "They are very fine rooms all the same. What they really need is a good cleaning."

"I am afraid the servants take advantage of me," Phoebe

admitted with a wistful sigh. "I find it so difficult to be *forceful* with them. Perhaps you will do better."

"Perhaps," Susannah said vaguely. "We have not had a great number of servants for me to practice on."

"No, I suppose not. You are so young, too." She giggled suddenly. "I hope you will not be offended, Susannah, but when Ivor told us he was marrying Miss Grainly, I thought at first he meant *Lucy*. After all, they practically grew up together. Even Horace was surprised—he could not picture you as a grown-up young lady."

It was the opening Susannah had been waiting for. "I am not offended in the least, your grace," she said, choosing her words carefully. "It is a natural assumption to make. In fact, it is my belief that both Lucy and Westbridge would be much happier if things were so circumstanced."

Phoebe opened her large brown eyes wide. "Do you think so? Then why did Ivor offer for *you*?"

"I rather think that I was offered to him, and not the other way around," Susannah said ruefully. "As far as I know, the entire idea was hatched up by my father and grandmother between them."

"Yes, and it would be just like Ivor to go along with it without stopping to think," Phoebe commented. "He is lazy about that sort of thing. Why, it took him three years to come around to asking someone on his own, and then he was thrown over." She sat down upon a chair, arranging the dust cover behind her until she was comfortable, then regarded Susannah thoughtfully. "And what about *you*? Would you, too, be happier if Ivor married Lucy?"

"Indescribably," Susannah said with conviction.

"Well, this is a fine state of affairs," Phoebe said cheerfully.

"Please do not think ill of me," Susannah begged. "I

would have refused him at the start if I had known then that Lucy was in love with him—and that I could never love him.''

"*Is* Lucy in love with him?" Phoebe asked with interest.

"I am sure of it."

"Then *that's* all right. At least someone loves him. Poor Ivor! He will have quite a history of being thrown over. He will need some comforting from one such as Lucy.''

"Then you think I should throw him over?" Susannah asked.

"Yes, certainly. Under the circumstances, it appears to be the most sensible thing to do—but not directly, of course. We must go about this delicately, else Ivor will end up permanently scarred and not wish to marry *anyone*, and where would that leave poor Lucy?''

"Just what I thought myself," Susannah said eagerly, "but I have been racking my brains for two weeks now and have come up with nothing at all.'' She sighed.

"Do not be despondent, Susannah. We will think of something. You did well to confide in me—I do so love a conspiracy!'' She actually clapped her hands with delight. "As I see it, we must make Ivor think it is his own idea—men prefer it that way, the silly creatures. Thank goodness we have plenty of time—your wedding is not until January at the earliest, or so your grandmother said last night.''

Susannah's face fell. "I would rather we settled this as quickly as possible," she said. "It is so awkward for me with grandmamma making plans and Ivor sending me gifts.''

"Yes, I see what you mean," Phoebe nodded. Then she brightened. "I am not really much good at intrigue, but I will do my best. I was so afraid this was going to be a *dull* summer!''

"Thank you, your grace," Susannah said.

"You really must call me Phoebe. Even if I am not to be your stepmamma-in-law, we will be co-conspirators, and I do think that is a much cosier relationship, don't you?''

Susannah merely smiled gratefully.

Susannah was delighted that she had found an ally in the duchess, but as the days went on she began to wonder if their alliance would be productive of anything but the most intricate and fantastic romances. As Susannah had done, Phoebe looked for ideas on the pages of novels. The Westham library was much more extensive than the one at Birchwood, so she had a much richer store of plots to draw from.

"A constant theme seems to be that the hero rescues the lady from a wicked villain," Phoebe told Susannah confidentially one day, after another tea in the morning room. "Generally, the lady is rescued from a tall tower, with no doorways and only one window." She sighed regretfully. "They do not seem to have anything like that in England— all those sort of castles are in Spain. I don't suppose we could visit Spain? Ivor knows the country well. I am sure he could tell us where to find a tower of the type we require."

"A trip to Spain seems unlikely at this time," Susannah said as diplomatically as she could, "nor do we have handy a villain to imprison Lucy there."

Phoebe giggled. "I expect we could get Smollett for that role," she said. "He has the look of a villain, with his dark eyes and all those teeth. He is rather young, though, and he ought to be bearded. Beards are not at all the fashion now. I doubt we could convince him to grow one."

Susannah seemed unable to impress upon her co-conspirator her desire for speed, especially as she was forthcoming with no reason for this desire beyond a general awkwardness in the situation as it now stood. Indeed, at one point Phoebe even suggested that they might simply let nature take her course, for that lengendary lady appeared to be leading things in the right direction all by herself.

Lucy always joined Susannah on her daily visits to Westham Park and played for hours upon the pianoforte while Susannah hatched plots with the duchess or giggled over nonsense with the young earl or assisted the duke with plans for the fête. More often than not, Westbridge, who was slightly disapproving of the whole idea of the fête, would join Lucy on the piano bench and they would talk the afternoon away. Susannah did not know what they talked about, but she suspected it was dull and erudite; often Ivor would leave Lucy's side long enough to fetch a book from the library and they would then pore over this together, reading passages aloud to each other and sometimes arguing in a strenuous but educated manner.

Of course, Westbridge did not spend all his time with his fiancée's aunt. He and Susannah soon made a habit of taking a morning ride together at least four days in the week. To her surprise, Susannah discovered that she could almost come to like the man, if only she didn't have to marry him. He told her much about the history of the Westhams, and as it was a very old family and Westbridge was very knowledgeable about it, they seldom lacked interesting conversation. But it was always a very one-sided conversation, with Westbridge lecturing and Susannah listening, making appropriate comments when they were required or asking a pertinent question now and then.

Often she found herself staring at Westbridge, studying him carefully, as if to fully convince herself that she did not wish to marry him. He was undoubtedly a handsome man, with classic but severe features; he wore his clothes beautifully and sat his horse well. Occasionally a smile would flit across his face, relieving his usual grave expression, but this occurred seldom. It was not a face made for laughter; indeed, Susannah could not recall ever having heard him laugh, except for a polite chuckle that was more like a cough. She knew she could never feel completely at ease with him; he was proud, unbending, and, worst of all, he missed the points of jokes. A serious outlook on life was often considered an asset in a man who had to make his way in the world, but Lord Westbridge already had position, power, and wealth—surely he could afford a little levity.

Susannah received her lesson in recent Westham history not from Westbridge but from Lord Fenworth. At last her curiosity was satisfied about that black sheep Ingram on a rainy afternoon while Smollett was abed with a chill, Lucy and Ivor intent over Shakespeare's sonnets, and Phoebe quietly dozing on the sofa.

Richard finished his tale in hushed tones, and Susannah was aware of a vague feeling of disappointment.

"Then he didn't kill anyone?" she asked. "I heard he murdered at least a dozen men and strangled two women."

"Treason is a far worse crime than murder," Richard said importantly, "and the closest he came to strangling women was when he almost married my mother."

"Truly?" Susannah asked breathlessly.

"They say he had a way with women," he told her,

unsure what the expression meant precisely. "He wrote them poetry and things. My mother sets great store by that sort of nonsense, although she really doesn't understand it. Now, *you're* all right, Susannah. I notice you don't let Ivor recite poetry to you like he does to poor old Lucy. I wonder you let him get away with it."

"What do you mean?" she asked.

"I admit I don't know very much about it, but aren't you supposed to be jealous of that sort of thing?"

"Oh, I don't mind," Susannah said truthfully.

"I knew it!" Richard exclaimed, then quickly lowered his voice again, for he did not wish to disturb his sleeping mother or attract the attention of the other two across the room. "You are trying to make Lucy marry Ivor, aren't you?"

"Whyever should you think that?" Susannah said, casting a nervous glance toward the couple in question.

"Now, don't play the innocent with *me*, Susannah," Richard said. "I heard you and mamma talking yesterday when you thought I was still out with Smollett."

"Why, you little sneak!" Susannah hissed in a loud whisper. "Weren't you ever taught it is not polite to listen through keyholes?"

"Actually, the door was open. Don't worry, Sukey, I shan't tell old Ivor about it. Truth to tell, I can see in a minute why you don't wish to marry him, although I think it's rather underhanded to push him off on your aunt."

"You are a fine one to talk about being underhanded," Susannah said, amused in spite of herself. "In future, it would be best if you minded your own business."

Richard sniffed. "If you feel that way about it, I shan't tell you the idea I had."

"You have had an idea? To help me, you mean?"

Richard nodded. "But I shan't tell you now. I must mind my own business."

"You wicked, wicked boy!" Susannah exclaimed, and was prepared to wheedle it out of him, but Richard said "hush" and nodded significantly.

Lucy and Westbridge were approaching them, having finished their discussion.

"Sukey, I almost forgot to tell you that I am going to the vicarage tomorrow morning to help Mrs. Gregg make tea cosies for the fête. Would you care to join me? We can use all the extra hands we can obtain."

Susannah made a little moué of distaste. "I would love to, Aunt Lu, but I am engaged to go riding tomorrow with Ivor. Isn't that right, Ivor?"

"I would certainly understand if you wished to break our engagement to help Lucy and Mrs. Gregg out, my dear," Westbridge said graciously. "After all, it is only a week until the fête, and they must have a great deal to do to prepare for it."

"But I would much rather go riding with you," Susannah insisted. "I am not very good at making tea cosies."

"That is true enough," Lucy said with a little laugh.

"Besides, there would be no one to bear Phoebe company if we are all off preparing for the fête," Susannah finished decisively. "You will be gone tomorrow afternoon with your father, and that will leave poor Phoebe with no one to help her with *her* plans."

Phoebe stirred at the sound of her name, opened her eyes, and continued the speech she had been making before she dozed off, as if there had been no interruption, "And we must have potted rabbit too. I do so love potted rabbit."

The others regarded her blankly for a moment until

Susannah laughed, "She is still planning the tea we will have in the summer house before the fête."

Westbridge gave a small smile, then offered to escort the two ladies home.

During all this time, Susannah had not forgotten the conversation she had overheard outside her father's door; in fact, she had spent many hours pondering its significance. The conclusion that Sandy had asked Sir Basil if he might pay court to Susannah was an easy and obvious one to make; not so obvious was why Sandy thought such a request might be acceptable, coming as it did from a poor tenant farmer. Susannah remembered her earlier suspicions that Sandy MacDougal was really a gentleman in disguise. These suspicions did not seem so outrageous any longer, especially when she recalled how Sandy spoke in a more educated accent during times of stress, as if that were the speech that came to him naturally, instead of the exaggerated Scottish burr he adopted at other times.

She longed to confront him with her suspicions, to discover the secret behind his mysterious past, but as long as she was engaged to Westbridge, this was impossible. She was never alone; she was always accompanied by Lucy or Will Tucker or Westbridge himself. Her patience was beginning to wear thin, and she was afraid that if her engagement were not broken off soon, she would do something rash and desperate.

Therefore she was most anxious to hear Richard's plan the next day. She went for her morning ride with Westbridge as usual but paid little attention to his discourse on the third duke, who came to a sorry end after opposing Cromwell. It seemed like days instead of only an hour later when she finally rode into the Westham stable yard behind Westbridge.

"I am sorry I cannot join you for tea today," Westbridge told her as he helped her to dismount, "but as you know, I promised my father I would ride to the church green with him this afternoon so we can examine the site for the fête with Mr. Gregg. Indeed, I would be happy to escort you to the vicarage if you have changed your mind about joining Lucy there."

"Thank you, Ivor, but Phoebe expects me," Susannah said, then added playfully. "Perhaps *you* can help Lucy with her tea cosies." Receiving only a blank stare in response to this, she went on with a little sigh, "Do not be concerned about me, Ivor. Phoebe and I always have much to talk about—planning for the fête, of course."

"Very well, then," he said. "I will meet you again tomorrow morning. Good day, Susannah."

Phoebe was in the morning room, and Susannah burst in on her breathlessly.

"Where is Richard?" she asked.

"Well, I like that," Phoebe said sulkily. "Not even so much as a 'good morning' or a 'how are you feeling today?' Just 'where's Richard,' as if my company were not enough for you."

"Don't be cross, Phoebe," Susannah said, removing her gloves and hat and tossing them onto a chair. "But has Richard not told you? He has thought of a plan for us."

Phoebe brightened. "The *clever* boy! I will send for him immediately. Ring the bell for me, Susannah. I am too comfortable to get up."

Richard arrived a few minutes later and was greeted by two pairs of hopeful brown eyes.

"Well?" Susannah prompted.

"That is a hole in the ground," Richard said with a grin, and easily ducked the cushion Susannah hurled at him.

"Don't be a beastly boy!" she exclaimed with a laugh. "You know perfectly well why we have called you in here. Now, let us hear your plan."

Richard settled himself leisurely on the settee and regarded them both in a lofty manner. "It appears quite simple to me," he said. "We must get them alone together somewhere and then surprise them. I think the summer house would do nicely for their rendezvous. It is fairly secluded and yet not so far out of the way as to make it difficult to lure them there."

"But how will that force Westbridge to break his engagement to *me*?" Susannah asked, puzzled. Her countrified upbringing had made her ignorant of the stricter conventions obtained in town, and she did not see how finding Lucy and Westbridge together in the summer house could lead to the conclusion she wished for.

"Why, don't you see?" Phoebe explained. "We will have found them in a compromising position. Oh, Dickie, you are such a clever boy!"

Richard smiled modestly.

"But if they are just standing there, chatting, that would not be very compromising," Susannah pointed out.

"Oh, it is compromising enough for our purposes," Phoebe assured her. "Many marriages have been made on much less than that. Of course, we will have to bring along reliable witnesses to find them there. Your grandmother, for instance, would be an excellent witness. I would depend upon her having a fit of the vapors upon discovering the two of them alone in the summer house." She giggled.

"I am quite sure she would," Susannah agreed, "but I cannot imagine how we could get her there. She has been complaining enough about going there for tea on Saturday afternoon, quite certain that the outside air will aggravate her arthritis. But I am quite sure she will enjoy herself once she is there," she added quickly, noticing Phoebe's look of consternation—to take high tea in the summer house was her idèa.

"I have already planned to move a comfortable chair there for her," Phoebe said defensively, "and there will be plenty of rugs to keep her warm. Oh dear, I wish she had said something when I made the invitation. I could have easily altered my plans, but now it is too late."

"Do not worry, Phoebe. I know she will be entirely comfortable—grandmamma *enjoys* complaining."

"Oh," Phoebe said without comprehension; she rarely complained about anything herself, and then only with just cause.

"I had rather thought Smollett would do nicely to discover them," Richard put in to distract his mother's thoughts from worries over her guests' comfort. "He is one of those people who is always commenting on the morals of others while forgetting to mind his own. And he has such an evil mind; he would be bound to make the worst of the situation."

"Dickie, you must not talk about poor Mr. Smollett that way," Phoebe said, for she never liked to believe anything bad about anyone of her acquaintance.

"I would rather not have Smollett in on our plans," Susannah said with an inadvertent shudder.

"He would not be *in* on it," Richard assured her. "We would merely use him as a dupe—to be present at the crucial moment."

"Very well," Susannah conceded, "but how are we to lure Lucy and Westbridge to the summer house in the first place?"

"That is where the real beauty of my plan shines through," Richard said with some pride. "We will send each of them a note with a plausible excuse for them to go there separately. If we do it on the same night as the fête, we can send Lucy to fetch something that was left there at teatime. I have not yet thought of what we would say in Ivor's note, though."

"Why not the same?" Phoebe suggested.

"Because Ivor would not go himself to fetch something," Richard explained patiently; he had already considered that idea while formulating his plan. "He would send me or Smollett or some handy servant, instead of going there himself."

"Perhaps we could send him a note from Lucy, requesting that he meet her there." This was Susannah's suggestion.

Richard shook his head. "That wouldn't work either. Ivor is too much a stickler for convention and would never go to meet Lucy unaccompanied. No, we must think of something better than that—something that will get him to the summer house right away, without anyone else knowing where he is going."

The three of them sat and thought, but no one could come up with anything that seemed even remotely plausible. Finally, Phoebe declared she was getting a headache from so much thinking and rang for tea, suggesting that refreshment might spur their creative instincts.

"I say, Susannah, you'll be pleased to know that the gypsies have arrived at last," Richard said presently, after his second slice of cake. "Ivor was grouching about their noise last night, but *I* don't mind. I am looking forward to having my fortune told again to see what they have to say about obstacles this time." He gave Susannah a knowing grin.

"A fortune teller is what we need right now," Susannah said with a laugh. "Perhaps she could advise us about what to say in the note."

Phoebe put her cup down with a clatter and stared at Susannah in a most disconcerting manner. "That is it! You have hit upon the very thing! Oh, I *knew* refreshment would help our mental powers, Susannah."

"What are you talking about?" she asked. She had mentioned the fortune teller in jest, not really thinking it would be of any use to them.

"Why, we must send Ivor a note saying that Dickie has been kidnapped by the gypsies, and Ivor must go to the summer house to pay them lots of money to get him back!" Phoebe said all in one breath, afraid that if she paused for air she would forget the idea as suddenly as she had thought of it.

"Kidnapped by gypsies!" Richard exclaimed delightedly. "That is a splendid idea, mamma!"

Phoebe flushed under this unaccustomed praise.

"Ivor hates those gypsies so," Richard continued enthusiastically. "I cannot think of anything that would send him running quicker. I suppose the gypsies will be quite willing to kidnap me for a few guineas," he added thoughtfully.

Phoebe's flush faded quickly. "But Dickie—I did not mean for you to actually be kidnapped!" she exclaimed, distressed. "Oh, no—that would be too terrible. I meant only that we should *say* that you were kidnapped in the note."

"But don't you think it would give an air of authenticity to the proceedings?" Richard asked hopefully.

"Do be quiet, Richard," Susannah put in. "Can't you see you are upsetting your mother? There is no need at all for you to be kidnapped in fact—just to say so is quite enough for our purposes."

"I suppose you are right," he admitted, taking another piece of cake for consolation. "Now, as I see it," he continued presently, licking some crumbs from his fingers, "we must have a definite plan of action for the night, a time schedule that we stick to faithfully. For instance, it wouldn't do to give Ivor a note telling him I had been kidnapped if he could see plainly that I was enjoying myself at cockshies or something. I will have to go off and hide *before* he gets the note. That means getting rid of Smollett for a while until we need him as a witness."

"I am sure you will think of something, Dickie," his mother said, "as long as it does not involve paying gypsies to kidnap people." She was quite done in by her single stroke of genius, and in a few minutes she had quietly dozed off while Susannah and Richard worked out the details of their plan.

"I say, Sukey," Richard remarked when everything appeared to be arranged satisfactorily, "what is to become of *you* when Ivor marries Lucy? I was rather looking forward to having you in the family."

"Why, thank you, Richard. That is very kind of you to say." Susannah smiled. "I will still be part of the family, though. Lucy is my aunt, after all."

"Yes, but it is not quite the same." He brightened suddenly. "Look here, you wouldn't care to wait a few years until I am old enough to marry you, would you? It would save me the trouble of looking around."

"I appreciate your offer, Richard, but I already have other plans for myself." She was touched by his proposal, though it was hardly more graceful than Ivor's had been.

"Well, no harm in asking," he said complacently, taking the last piece of cake.

✂❀ CHAPTER TEN ❀✂

THE FIRST DAY of the fête began with threatening clouds in the sky, and the residents of Duxtonbury watched them anxiously, fearful that the festivities of the weekend would be spoiled by rain. To everyone's relief, the sky was clear by noontime; the clouds had dispersed after one brief, futile little shower. Preparations on the church green proceeded apace.

Cooking gear was set up to produce such delicacies as grilled sausages and roasted chestnuts for the revelers, alongside long tables filled with pies and tarts and meat pastries of every description. Half a dozen barrels of ale were rolled up from the inn; lemonade would also be provided for the ladies and children. On another table, Mrs. Gregg proudly displayed the fruits of her labors, the price of each item neatly marked on white cards. She and her ladies had been industrious; there were tea cosies, pot holders, mufflers and mittens, carpet slippers, and babies' booties and saques to sell for the benefit of the church. Mrs. Maggins had donated odds and ends of ribbons and lace, and these had been crafted into book markers and pen wipers of every shape and color. Most of the pen wipers would be offered as prizes to the winners of spin-the-wheel or cockshies, but those who were less lucky at these games could purchase one from Mrs. Gregg for a ha'penny.

Nearby, enclosures had been set up to contain cattle, sheep, and pigs. The judging of the animals and the award-ing of ribbons to the best livestock was a highlight of the fête, especially since a prize-winning animal fetched a better price at market. The farmers' wives, meanwhile, had their own competition; many had been cooking for weeks, preparing pickalillie, jams, jellies, and pickles. The duke of Duxton himself would sample these offerings and judge them for excellence; indeed, it was his favorite part of the whole affair.

At the far end of the green, the gypsies went ahead with their own preparations, hauling a number of their brightly painted caravans from the East Meadow to house the jugglers and dancers, and setting up a tent for fortune telling. Many of the good wives of Duxtonbury viewed this operation with disapproval, but did not voice any open objection. While the gypsies would not donate their pro-ceeds to the church fund, the fortune telling and other entertainments they provided drew more people to the fête who while they were there might spend a sixpence on either a tea cosy in the shape of a thatched cottage or a warm woolen muffler knitted by Mrs. Stark.

The duke, Westbridge, and the vicar were much in evidence during the morning, directing the placement of the tables and kiosks, checking the honesty of the games of chance, or helping a farmer lead a balky pig into a pen. Many of the townspeople came out to help just to catch sight of the duke, for they had little opportunity otherwise to do so. It gave them a certain pleasure, a remnant of their feudal past, when the duke addressed them by name and asked after their families, remembering even those who did not live on the Westham estate. "What a kind man," they would remark to one another proudly, "not at all pushed up by his own consequence. Fancy his asking after my Daisy, who has been in service in London these three years and more."

At two in the afternoon the duke officially opened the celebration by making a little speech and springing a great surprise—the pantomime would perform there tomorrow evening, and admission was free to all. This was greeted with loud huzzahs and applause. Then Mr. Gregg said his little piece and led them in a prayer to the effect that they would not forget to be generous while they enjoyed themselves; the purpose of the fête was, after all, to earn money for the church and thus contribute to the greater glory of God Himself. There was some shuffling in the audience as he came to the part of his text that dealt with temperance, and Sam Larkin had to be hushed for making a rude comment. It was already too late for *him* to profit from such a lecture.

Naturally, the two misses Grainly were excluded from these opening ceremonies, but they were subjected to their own lecture from Lady Grainly, who touched on many of the same points as the vicar. She reminded them, too, that it was only with reluctance that she allowed them to attend the fête at all; they were at all times to remember who they were—that is, the ladies of Birchwood Hall, who must always keep in mind the precepts she had given them to live by.

The Westham pony trap arrived at a quarter to three to take all the Grainlys to tea at the summer house. Lady Grainly grumbled continously under her breath about the rude informality of the occasion and how distressing it was to eat out-of-doors what with the insects and the unhealthful breezes. But even her grandmother's constant carping could not dampen Susannah's high spirits. Today was the day! By this time tomorrow she would be free. She actually reached over and squeezed Lucy's hand briefly, wishing she could tell her aunt how very wonderful her life would soon become. Lucy gave her a puzzled glance but returned the gesture affectionately.

The summer house was no more than a round platform with a roof supported by Grecian-style pillars. There was a wooden seat along the circumference of the inside wall that was too uncomfortable to sit on for very long, but cushions and rugs had been scattered across the floor, and the guests made themselves comfortable on these. Phoebe had supervised the arrangements and was quite pleased with the result, but while she was scatterbrained, she was not thoughtless. As she had promised Susannah, a single armchair was provided for Lady Grainly's comfort, and there she sat, well wrapped in rugs, overlooking all the others from her superior height.

"Are you all ready to go ahead?" Lord Fenworth asked Susannah in a conspiratorial whisper as he munched on jam and bread.

Susannah glanced around, then nodded. "I have the notes here." She indicated her bodice. "I was up half the night writing Lucy's, for she would recognize my grandmother's hand." She giggled nervously, "If the plan fails to work, I can always make my living by forgery."

Richard nodded, satisfied. "I've got mamma all primed. I do hope she remembers what she must do. We've been over it a dozen times."

"What are you two whispering about?" Westbridge asked, lowering himself onto a cushion beside them while balancing a plate full of food and a teacup.

"Nothing," Susannah said quickly, and catching Richard's eye, they laughed together.

Westbridge wiped his chin quickly, wondering if he had spilled some crumbs there, but all seemed to be in order.

"I have received permission from your grandmother to escort both you and Lucy to the fête," he told Susannah.

"Lucy has already promised to help Mrs. Gregg sell her tea cosies," Susannah replied, "so you needn't worry about her. But I am quite anxious to enjoy *everything*." She nearly giggled again as Richard did a fair imitation of the gesturing of a fortune teller behind Westbridge's back. "Will you buy me a fairing, Ivor?" she asked.

"We will see," he said. "Perhaps only to support the cause of the church fund."

"But not to please me," Susannah could not resist adding.

"You must know, Susannah, that my only thought is to please you," Westbridge said with that same hint of reproach she had heard often before.

Susannah frowned slightly as Richard continued to gesture behind his stepbrother's back. "I promised Richard that he could come with us," Susannah said.

"Is he not going with Smollett?" Westbridge asked, arching an eyebrow.

"I would much rather go with you, Ivor," Richard put in.

Westbridge turned his head around to regard the boy with something approaching tenderness. "Very well, Richard, but you must promise not to wander off."

Susannah choked on her tea, and instantly Westbridge was all solicitation for her well-being.

After the servants cleared away the tea things, the duchess appeared ready to take her husband's arm to walk the short distance back to the house, until she noticed her son gesturing wildly.

"Oh, I nearly forgot!" Phoebe exclaimed. "Mr. Smollett, would you mind coming back to the house with me? I hate to spoil your fun, but I need your help with some correspondence that cannot be put off." She fluttered her eyelashes at him, and, as had been planned, this was more than enough to convince him to abandon any plans he had had for attending the fête.

"Certainly, your grace," he said smoothly, wondering only a little at her request.

"It will only take a short time—until about *seven o'clock*, I should think," Phoebe continued, proud that she had remembered her part so well. Richard and Susannah both breathed a silent sigh of relief.

"Susannah, I will expect you home no later than eight o'clock," Lady Grainly told her granddaughter as Sir Basil helped her into the trap, 'and you, too, Lucy. It has been my experience at events of this kind that the common people are in a position to drink far more ale than they are accustomed to, and as the hour progresses they become more rowdy."

"You may depend upon me to bring them both home safely," Westbridge assured her. Susannah caught Richard's eye again, and they both giggled—if their little plan progressed as scheduled Westbridge might have some trouble carrying out this promise. Things had already begun smoothly with the removal of Smollett from their party.

Once they reached the church green, Lucy joined Mrs. Gregg at her table as she had arranged, and Susannah attempted to divert Westbridge's attention long enough for Richard to make good his escape. This was more difficult than she had anticipated, for Westbridge had no notion of frivolity; indeed, he appeared to have made a grim resolution not to be diverted at any cost. He frowned upon her playing spin-the-wheel, considering it a baser form of gambling, and turned his nose up at the little items for sale, claiming he could obtain better quality goods in London, and if she really desired a book marker, he had several leather ones of his own to spare and would be pleased to give them to her. When she reminded him of his desire to help out the church fund, he threw a few shillings into the plate without taking anything in return. Mrs. Gregg was very grateful; Susannah was not.

After a while they were attracted by the sound of music from the gypsies' area and strolled over to watch them dance. When Susannah tore her attention away from this exhilarating spectacle after some ten minutes, Richard was nowhere to be seen.

Westbridge did not notice his stepbrother's disappearance for quite some time. At last he took Susannah away from the dancers, claiming it was quite inappropriate for her to view and he was ashamed he had remained there so long with her. She asked him to buy her a jam tart, but this he refused also, surprised she should be hungry so soon after their enormous tea. They wandered about aimlessly, stopping now and then to chat with an acquaintance. Susannah had never thought until now that one could be bored at a fête.

"What has become of Richard?" Westbridge asked at last, looking around.

"I don't know," Susannah replied with little concern.

"It is too bad of him to wander off, after he expressly promised he would not," Westbridge said crossly.

"I expect he has gone to watch the jugglers. He has a great fondness for them," Susannah said. "I shouldn't worry about him, Ivor. I don't see how he can come to any harm."

"Still, he did promise," Westbridge insisted, searching the crowd for any sign of the errant youth.

"What is the time, Ivor?" Susannah asked, hoping to draw his attention away to other things.

He took out his pocket watch and consulted it. "Twenty past the hour," he said. "When did you last see him? Perhaps we can retrace our steps."

Susannah ignored this remark, for the time had come for the next step in the plan. She suspected she would have some difficulty with it, considering Westbridge's general disagreeableness. She was not mistaken.

"Ivor, never mind about Richard," she said. "I should dearly love to have my fortune told."

Westbridge frowned with disapproval. "I do not think it is a good idea to encourage these people to tell their lies," he said. "Especially when they demand silver from you for their falsehoods."

"There is no harm in it, Ivor," she pleaded. "If they do tell lies, they are usually very pretty ones, and I do not begrudge the shilling they request."

He smiled briefly. "I would be happy to tell your fortune myself, my dear. It would be at least as accurate as anything that heathen woman could tell you, and probably more so.''

"But that would not be the same at all," she insisted. "Lucy and I both had our fortunes told last year, and even my grandmother made no objection." Her brown eyes were melting and Ivor began to waver.

"Your aunt had her fortune told as well?" he asked.

"Of course! She saw no harm in it either." Susannah sighed wistfully. "Please, Ivor, I shall not bother you for anything else if only you will allow me this."

Still he resisted, and Susannah forged on, beginning to get a little desperate as the minutes ticked by. "It will take only a few minutes, Ivor, and you can wait for me right outside."

"Very well," he gave in at last, for he could see she was determined to have her way. "But do not give her more than a shilling—she will be stealing that from you as it is."

"Thank you, Ivor," she exclaimed with feeling.

Just as she had predicted, the woman filled her head with pretty lies. Of course, it was quite worth the shilling to experience the exotic atmosphere inside the tent, which was like nothing Susannah had ever seen elsewhere. The walls were hung with red and black draperies, the floor covered with patterned rugs, the smoky fragrance of incense filled the room. The woman herself was dressed colorfully and the innumerable bracelets she wore jingled and clanked musically as she dealt out her tattered and dirty cards in order to unlock the secrets of the future.

A few minutes later Susannah emerged from the tent, breathless and excited.

"Well, was it worth it?" Westbridge asked her impatiently.

"She said I will marry and bear many children and live a long and happy life."

"There, you see! I could have told you the same thing and saved a shilling." He took her arm to lead her away from the gypsies before she had any other whimsical notions.

"But, Ivor, it is the most peculiar thing," she continued quickly, pulling away from him. "The woman told my fortune and then gave me this note to give to you." She handed him a slip of paper. "She said that you must not tell anyone of its contents, or you will regret the consequences."

Westbridge creased his brows curiously as he took the note from her. "I expect they are worried that I won't allow them to continue to camp on the East Meadow when I am duke," he said, and opened the note to read it.

Susannah watched with bated breath as his look of impatience changed to one of thundering rage. He crumpled the note into a tight little ball as soon as he had read it through.

"This is outrageous!" he exclaimed.

"What is it?" Susannah asked, feigning the proper amount of curiosity.

"I cannot tell you, but something must be done about this immediately. Perhaps if you will allow me to escort you home—"

"Oh, no!" Susannah protested. "It is not even seven and I do not have to be home until eight."

"But Susannah, I cannot leave you here alone, and I must attend to this without delay."

"I can join Lucy at Mrs. Gregg's table," she said. "I will be quite safe there."

"Very well," he said reluctantly. "I will try to be back in time to escort you both back to the Hall by eight, as I promised.'' He left her side abruptly, striding in a purpose-ful way toward Westham Park. Susannah gave a laugh of sheer joy; he had taken the bait without question or demur and she could now continue with the next part of her plan.

"Where is Ivor?'' Lucy asked when Susannah joined her presently.

"He had some urgent business to attend to,'' she explained. "He said he would be back in time to see us home.''

A few minutes later, after she had sold a pair of baby's booties to Sally Jeffers, Susannah exclaimed, as though it had just come to mind, "Lucy, I nearly forgot! Will Tucker gave me this note a few minutes ago to give to you.'' She pulled out a second slip of paper from her bodice.

Lucy finished the transaction she was engaged in, then took the note from Susannah's hand. She read it and sighed.

"What is it?'' Susannah asked.

"Mamma has left her shawl at the summer house and wishes me to go and fetch it,'' she said. "I do not understand, though—why did Will not give me the note himself? I could have fetched the shawl and returned by now.''

Susannah shrugged. "I suppose he saw me first and wished to deliver the note before he forgot about it completely. You know how scatterbrained he is.''

"I suppose so,'' Lucy said with another sigh. "I may as well go and fetch the wretched thing now. I won't be long—but, Susannah, do promise me you won't go off on your own.''

"I will stay here and help Mrs. Gregg,'' Susannah promised, and had every intention of so doing, at least until Smollett showed his face and she could proceed with the next part of the plan. But a few minutes later, a familiar bright head approached the table and inquired how much, please, for this wee pair o' carpet slippers.

Susannah looked up with delight, her heart rising in her throat. "Sandy!" she cried. "How lovely to see you."

"Hush now, lassie," he warned as Mrs. Gregg eyed them suspiciously. "Ye dinna want t' start the tongues t' waggin' now, do ye? Just sell me this pair o' slippers. There's a guid lass."

"I don't care if they do wag," Susannah said recklessly. "Mrs. Gregg, you have met Sandy MacDougal, have you not?"

Mrs. Gregg allowed that she had.

"My father has sent Sandy to escort me tonight," Susannah continued, "so I am afraid I must leave you now, Mrs. Gregg."

"Well, I thank you kindly for your help, Susannah," Mrs. Gregg said, her suspicions in no way allayed.

"You're a sly one, there's nae doobt o' that," Sandy told her as she took his arm.

"You must buy me a fairing," she said. "I absolutely insist."

"Weel now, miss," he said, looking about self-consciously to see who might be observing them. "Surely yer betrothed maun hae bought ye a fairin' himself?"

"No, he has not. He refuses to spend money on anything. Now, come along, Sandy. The gypsies are selling much nicer things than these—little carved animals and such. I rather fancy a little badger I saw."

"Troth, if yer father wad come here and spy us together, he'd be sair pressed, ye ken weel—t' say naught o' yer betrothed himself."

"Sandy, you know I cannot make heads or tails of what you are saying when you talk like that," Susannah laughed.

He shook his head ruefully. "Aye, there's no gettin' round you, is there, lassie? Very well, I'll buy you a fairin' if that's what you desire."

Not only did he buy her the little carved badger, but in the space of only a few minutes he bought her two sizzling sausages, a jam tart, a tiny basket of potpourri, and even allowed her to play spin-the-wheel.

On her third try at this game of chance she won a pen wiper shaped like an owl, which she presented to him ceremoniously.

"Hout nae, what's an ignorant, ill-educated brute like me goin' t' do wi' yon pen wiper?" he teased, reverting to his strongest burr.

Susannah flushed. "My father should not have repeated that to you," she said, then shyly, "but you should know how I really feel about you, Sandy."

"Aye, I've a fair idea," he admitted. For a moment they caught each other's eyes and seemed to be enclosed in their own little bubble as the rest of the world faded away to nothingness. Sandy, seeing the danger, quickly brought them out of it.

"Now then, do you fancy havin' your fortune told, lass?"

"I have had it told already, but the gypsy woman couldn't tell me what I most wanted to know. Only you can tell me that, Sandy."

"And what might that be, lassie?"

"I think you know," she said. "I overheard rather a lot of what you and my father were discussing in his office that day, and it has made me wonder exceedingly. For instance, what reason does my father have to be grateful to you?''

"That's plain enough, I should think," he replied without meeting her eyes. "I've taken over a farm no one else would have and planted on it again."

"Yes, that is true," Susannah agreed with amusement. "And you were only *pretending* to pull up your carrots for weeds that day and you are really an *excellent* farmer any landlord would be grateful to have.

"Aye, that's it," he said with a twinkle.

"So good a farmer are you that you dared ask permission to court the master's daughter."

"Aye, and was refused, as you must know with your big ears."

"There is no reason to make personal remarks," Susannah said pertly. "I am only trying to discover the truth."

"Always supposin' there's a truth to discover."

"Can you deny it?"

He hesitated slightly, then admitted, "Nae, I canna. But I am afraid to tell you, lass. I kenna how you'll take to it."

"Nothing you could tell me would change my mind about you," she assured him fervently. "It would not matter to me if you were penniless or a highwayman or—" She searched her mind for something even more terrible, but before she could come up with it, they were interrupted.

"Ah, Miss Grainly, how pleasant to see you. I have lost Lord Fenworth somewhere. Her grace sent me to find him and fetch him home, but he is nowhere to be seen."

"Smollett!" Susannah exclaimed, suddenly remembering her plan. "You have come at last!"

Smollett was mightily pleased by this indication of her

regard for him. He smiled toothily and said, "Indeed, I could not tear myself away from her grace any sooner, but had I known you were awaiting me I certainly would have tried."

"Oh dear, what is the time?" Susannah asked, distressed that she could have forgotten so completely the part she had to play. "We must find Richard immediately. I think he has gone to the summer house. Let us go there now and look for him."

"To the summer house?" Smollett asked. "That sounds unlike him when there is a juggler who is spinning flaming torches. I fancy we would do better to seek his lordship there."

"No, no, I am quite sure he is in the summer house," she insisted.

"If he is, he will come to no harm," Smollett said smoothly. "I would much rather enjoy this little fête with you, Miss Grainly. Oh, excuse me, I don't believe I know your friend." He looked at Sandy and blinked. "Why, yes, of course I know him. Grainly, isn't it? Alexander Grainly? We were at university together. Alfred Smollett." He held out his hand and Sandy took it before he could think or he surely would have denied the acquaintance.

"Of course," Smollett went on, unaware of Susannah's dropped jaw and Sandy's extreme discomfort. "I should have made the connection before—you must be related to Miss Grainly here. A cousin, perhaps?"

"Perhaps," Sandy admitted with a groan, then without looking at Susannah again, he said, "Why don't you and Miss Grainly go ahead without me? I must be off."

"Well," Smollett said, disgruntled by his abrupt departure. "He was always such a pleasant chap at university. I suppose wealth always makes a man uppity, though. It's a sad thing." He turned to Susannah eagerly, glad of the opportunity to be alone with her. "Now, Miss Grainly, I have long hoped for an occasion to speak to you alone. There is much we can discuss. Let us have a nice ramble and chat together."

But Susannah made no answer save a quick "excuse me," and left his side as abruptly as Alexander Grainly had, making off in the same direction.

❦ CHAPTER ELEVEN ❧

LORD WESTBRIDGE PACED back and forth across the small floor of the summer house in a towering fury. He had told his father time and again that no good would come of allowing those heathen gypsies on their land—now he was proven right! But at what a cost! Not content with stealing two or three sheep and a dozen or so chickens each year, in addition to being well fed out of the pantry of Westham Park and making a fortune at the fête with their hocus-pocus and claptrap, the bloody heathens had now insulted the very person of nobility. They had taken Lord Fenworth and were holding him hostage.

The note indicated that a member of their wicked band would come to the summer house at half past seven to collect three hundred guineas for the safe return of Lord Fenworth. Three hundred guineas, indeed! As if he had that sum lying about in gold, awaiting such an emergency.

Ivor was determined that the gypsies would be paid not in gold but in lead and had stopped at Westham Park only long enough to fetch a good, stout pistol. He would lie in wait at the summer house until their henchman came at the appointed time, then Ivor would show him how a Westham defended his own against the nefarious deeds of evildoers. The Westham honor would be avenged!

He paused in his pacing to check his watch again. It was only ten past seven; he had twenty minutes more to wait, plenty of time to conceal himself in the most advantageous hiding place as soon as he decided where that would be. It was years since he had planned a battle formation, but it was a skill one did not lose. Even as he paced he was assessing the situation, examining the surrounding bushes to determine the most likely approach the foe would take, searching the deepening shadows for a place where a man might hide unseen, ready to attack that foe.

He heard a rustle in the bushes and was immediately alert, all his senses finely tuned. Their messenger was early—hoping to catch him off-guard, no doubt—but Ivor was ready. He quickly concealed himself behind one of the supporting pillars and awaited his moment.

A soft step sounded on the floor of the summer house, and Ivor sprung out from his hiding place, grabbing the villain strongly and looking about for more. A moment later he realized his mistake.

"Lucy!" he exclaimed. "Whatever are you doing here?"

"I might well ask you the same thing, Ivor," Lucy said. "Pray unhand me."

Ivor released her and stepped back, then Lucy noticed the pistol in his hand.

"What is going on?" she asked, her eyes widening.

"Why do you have that?" She pointed to the pistol as if it were a poisonous viper about to spring.

"This is no place for you, Lucy," he said. "I must ask you to leave here quickly."

"I shan't leave until you have given me an explanation," Lucy said, rubbing her arm where Ivor had grabbed it. "I came here to find mamma's shawl, only to discover you lurking about with that—that *gun*."

"It is a pistol," Ivor said precisely. "I cannot give you any explanation—to do so might be dangerous for both of us. I suggest you find your mother's shawl and leave again as quickly as possible."

Lucy glanced around but could not discover the missing shawl. "It does not seem to be here."

"Doubtless it was bundled up with the rugs and taken back to the Park," Ivor said impatiently, "I will make sure it is sent back to you tomorrow. Now go—quickly, while it is still light. There is no time to be lost." He tried to push her on her way, but Lucy stood her ground firmly.

"No, Ivor," she said with determination. "I *will* know what is happening before I leave here."

"If I tell you, will you promise to go straight home and mention to no one you have seen me here?"

"I can make no such promise. If you are in danger, Ivor, let me go for help."

"No! I must do this on my own!" He realized that he was almost shouting and checked himself, consulting his watch again. Only ten minutes were left before his fateful appointment. "You must go now, Lucy. There is no time for further argument."

"I will not!" she declared, seating herself firmly on one of the benches that lined the walls. "Is it a duel, Ivor?"

she asked with mounting alarm. "Is that why you are so insistent upon being alone?"

"No, nothing like that," he told her, then seeing that nothing short of an explanation or physical force would move her, he decided upon the former. "If you must know, I have received a note saying that Richard has been kidnapped by the gypsies," he told her quickly. "They are coming here at half past seven to exchange him for a sum of money. It is essential that I meet them alone. If they see that I am accompanied, they will turn away and Richard will be kept in their hands until they arrange another rendezvous."

Lucy had gasped several times during this narrative, glad that she was sitting, for her legs had gone weak, and there was a queer feeling in her stomach as she realized that Ivor was about to risk his life.

"Now will you go?" Ivor asked, a little desperately.

"Certainly not!" she said, gathering her strength. "I could not live with myself knowing I left you alone on this vigil. What if you are left wounded and cannot go for help?"

"I will be quite all right, I assure you. There is no sense in both of us putting ourselves into danger."

"Then there *is* a danger!" Lucy cried, anguished. "I refuse to go, Ivor. I will keep myself hidden unobtrusively, but I cannot leave you alone and bleeding."

Grudgingly, Ivor gave in, only because the time was growing too short.

"Very well," he said, taking her by the arm. "I will show you where you must hide." She stood where he positioned her, her head held high, her eyes shining. He paused for a moment and felt a reluctant admiration stir in him. She was behaving foolishly, but with great courage.

"You are a brave woman, Lucy Grainly," he said softly, then sought his own hiding place.

The minutes ticked by with an agonizing slowness, the only sound the soft rustle of the wind in the trees and a faint, eerie hint of some distant music. Ivor spared no thought for those who were enjoying that music at closer range; all his energies were keyed to watching the footpaths, keeping his body taut and ready to spring. Now and then he moved only enough to consult his watch in the fading light. Half past seven. Twenty-five to eight. Twenty to eight. Still the gypsy messenger did not appear. At a quarter to the hour, Ivor decided they had waited long enough.

"This is intolerable!" he declared, and his voice was so sudden and so loud that Lucy gave an involuntary scream.

"What is it?" he asked, rushing to her side. "What have you seen?"

"N-nothing," she said, shaking slightly. "You startled me, that is all."

"I should not have allowed you to remain here," he said. "Look at you. You are quivering like a leaf in the wind."

"It was not your decision to make," Lucy said, then suddenly lowered her eyes. "Unless you believe it was my presence that kept them away."

"No, no," he reassured her, tucking the pistol away in his coat pocket. "You were well hidden—even I had trouble detecting you at times. I do not know what has prevented them from keeping their appointment, but I propose to find out. However, first I will escort you home. I promised Lady Grainly to have you back by eight, and I can still keep that promise if we hurry."

"You must be sure and tell me when you have found

Richard again," Lucy said. "I will not be easy in my mind until I know he—and you—are safe and free from danger."

"Your concern does you credit, Lucy. Perhaps I should have listened to you before and allowed you to fetch help, for obviously we must start a search as soon as possible, beginning at the gypsy camp. There are so many hiding places in the woods that I fear it may be morning before I have any news for you." His voice gradually softened as he spoke, for he had just noticed how the setting sun illuminated Lucy's hair to make a halo around her face. Suddenly, he recalled a meeting they had had in this very place ten—no, it must be twelve years ago. How young they both had been then. He himself no more than a youth, untouched by the rigors of war and the buffetings of fate. Yet Lucy had spent the entire intervening time at Birchwood Hall and remained unchanged. For the first time in years he recalled the thrill that first tentative kiss had given him, recalled how exciting a mere kiss could be to one who was not used to the occupation, and unaccountably he longed to recapture that emotion, here in the same place, with the same girl, his first love.

Lucy waited patiently as he seemed to be working something out in his head; no doubt he was preparing a plan to rescue Richard from the heathens. Thus she was taken quite by surprise when he grasped her by the shoulders and pulled her close. Her heart leaped to her throat at this unexpected but most welcome attention, then she chided herself for a fool. No doubt he had heard a sound in the bushes and was desirous of protecting her.

But when he murmured her name tenderly, and bent his head to hers, she had no doubt any longer of his intentions. She met his lips gladly, and that one kiss she had lived on for so long, that she had thought was the only one she would ever receive, was finally repeated. Indeed, it was improved upon.

Ivor was surprised by the rush of feelings that coursed through him when he sensed the passion that hid behind Lucy's serene exterior. He was mistaken. Lucy *had* changed. Twelve years ago he had kissed a girl; now he kissed a woman, a woman who yielded sweetly and fearlessly to his touch—a woman he could never have, for he was promised to another.

"What a blind fool I have been, Lucy," he said, reluctantly breaking off the kiss but quickly following it up by a long series of kisses to her eyes, her cheeks, her hair, and again her lips. She received his attentions joyfully, returning them in kind.

"Ivor," she murmured, and again, "Ivor." She rested her head against his shoulder, enjoying the warmth of his breath against her ear when he murmured as tenderly as she, "Lucy."

"Why did I not discover you sooner?" he asked. "All these years, all this time, you were at Birchwood while I have been alone."

"You could have had me at any time, Ivor," she told him trustingly. "I have always belonged to you."

"And now that I have found you again, I cannot have you."

"Why not?" she asked, looking up into his face.

He stroked her cheek. "You know very well, my darling. I belong to another and cannot give my love freely."

"It is not too late to change that, Ivor. There is still time to break your engagement," Lucy said practically.

He shook his head regretfully. "I could not act so

dishonorably, so despicably. It would break Susannah's heart. I would not be able to live with myself afterwards."

"And what of *my* heart, Ivor?" Lucy argued forcefully. "Is it not more dishonorable to live a lie—married to one you do not love?" In the space of a few minutes she had received a taste of what her life could be like and how different it was from her spinsterhood at Birchwood Hall, always under her mother's thumb, never daring to show her true nature. With only a few kisses she had built herself a life beside the man she loved—had always loved—bearing him children, keeping him company even when old age made them both weak and helpless. She was not ready to give up this vision without a fight, not for her niece, whom she loved dearly, certainly not for such a nebulous notion as honor.

"Please do not tempt me, Lucy," he said, anguished. "It would be so easy to forsake honor and take you away with me now, this very minute. It would be easy, but not right. Ours are not the only lives that would be affected by such a decision.

Wisely, Lucy did not pursue the subject further for the moment. Her life had been spent waiting; she had learned the virture of patience. He would change his mind, she was sure, but not if she pressed him into it. Already she could see in his eyes that he was undecided, that his words about honor did not carry the full weight of conviction. She would be patient, as she always had been, and trust in the love that he had revealed to her.

He released her reluctantly and said, "I must get you home. We have wasted too much time here, and Richard is still in danger."

"Did you really think this was time wasted?" she asked softly.

"Not the last few minutes," he admitted, pressing her hand to his lips, "but we must try to forget this interlude, Lucy. It is best that we pretend it never happened."

"Of course, Ivor," she said, knowing she would never forget it and confident that he felt the same.

"Come," he said, tucking her hand under his arm. "We are late and must stop at the fête again in case Susannah is waiting for us."

They walked back to the church green wordlessly, their only communication the slight pressure of Ivor's hand again hers. That and the fact that the whole world seemed somehow different, more brightly tinted, more alive, more real, served to remind Lucy that what had just taken place in the summer house was not a product of her imagination, a fantasy of a long stifled passion, but had actually happened. Ivor loved her; she was as certain of that as if he had actually spoken the words aloud, and nothing would ever be the same again. Even the people at the fête seemed changed; they appeared kinder, more cheerful. Perhaps it was only the result of the vast quantities of ale they had been drinking, but Lucy was convinced it was because they all sensed her joy and exultation and shared in it.

Mrs. Gregg was a little surprised to see Lucy back again; she thought the girl would have been home by now. No, she did not know where Susannah was. She had not seen her for an hour and more. One of Sir Basil's tenants had been sent to escort her.

"Then she is probably safely at home already," Ivor told Lucy confidently, "and that is where we must get you."

But as they walked through the crowds again, they met Sir Basil, who was also seeking his daughter. They told him what Mrs. Gregg had said.

"I sent no tenant to escort her," Sir Basil said, a slight look of concern on his face.

Ivor and Lucy exchanged worried glances as thoughts of the gypsies sprang to both their minds. Ivor explained quickly to Sir Basil about the note he had received, but before he could finish, a cheerful voice greeted them.

"There you are! I have been looking all over for you. Well, is it all right? Did Susannah and Smollett find you at the summer house? What is the matter? Have I grown another head?"

"Richard!" Lucy cried, and gave the boy a sudden embrace. "We have been so worried about you!"

"Please, Lucy," Richard said, embarrassed. "People are looking."

"What happened? Were you to able to escape from them?" Lucy asked eagerly.

"Hasn't Susannah explained it all to you?" he asked.

"I have not seen Susannah since she gave me the note that told me you had been taken," Westbridge said sternly. "Perhaps you would care to explain, young man."

"Oh, *bother*," Richard muttered. Then, not caring to say more than he had to, for it was obvious by now things had not gone according to plan, he said, "It was only a joke, Ivor."

"A fine joke! We were about to call out search parties for you. Do you know what anguish you have caused this fine young lady? To say nothing of my own distress."

"Please, Ivor, perhaps we should not discuss it here," Lucy suggested, noticing that they were attracting attention. "Why don't you take me home and deal with Richard later?"

"Very well," Westbridge conceded, "but I warn you, young man, your little joke will cost you dearly."

"We may still need those search parties for Susannah," Sir Basil said grimly. He had begun to form some suspicions about the identity of the mysterious tenant Mrs. Gregg had mentioned and was growing more uneasy by the minute.

The four of them made for the footpath leading back to Birchwood Hall, but they had not walked very far before they came across a dark form huddled on the ground. Lucy gave a little scream, fearing it was Susannah herself, come to some dire pass in the shadows of the woods, but closer inspection proved it to be no other than Smollett. He was covered by a tweed coat and quite unconscious. It took them some time to bring him around.

"Was it the gypsies?" Westbridge asked him as soon as he seemed able to speak. The discovery that Richard's kidnapping had been a hoax had not lessened his suspicions against the heathens.

"Gypsies?" Smollett repeated groggily, then opened his eyes a little wider, taking in the countenances of his rescuers. "Sir Basil—your daughter—" he licked his lips and continued weakly, "I fear she is being ravished by that brute. I tried to stop him, but as you see, I was overpowered."

Smollett had been quite disconcerted to be left standing alone in the middle of the crowd. He glanced around in embarrassment and gladly noted that no one seemed to regard his discomfiture in the least. Then he, too, took off in the same direction.

"Miss Grainly," he said, catching up to her at the edge of the woods.

"Oh, what *is* it, Mr. Smollett? Can't you see that I am in a hurry?"

He gave her his toothy grin. "Now, you don't want to go chasing after your cousin. After all, he *is* your cousin, and you can see him any time you like. I would be very pleased if you would allow me to show you some of the delights of this fête. Perhaps you would care to play at spin-the-wheel." He tried to take her arm.

"I have already played spin-the-wheel," she said impatiently. "Do let me go, Mr. Smollett. I must talk to Sandy immediately. If you want to be any use at all"—a reminder of the plan she should now be executing came to her—"why don't you go to the summer house and fetch the shawl I left there? I would be very grateful if you would."

He hesitated, but this was too good an opportunity to pass up. "Miss Grainly, it is a warm night, you do not need your shawl. And if you should chance to be cold, I would be happy to warm you." He reached out to take her arm again, but she avoided him.

"You really *must* let me go to my cousin, Mr. Smollett," she said, and as he seemed to need further persuasion, she kicked him sharply upon the shin and took off down the path once more.

Smollett was left hopping about on one foot while he clutched the other in agony, and this time some people did notice his plight and giggled and pointed. This made Smollett angry. He had offered to escort Miss Grainly in a very polite manner, and she had rebuffed him most rudely. Well, he would show her that he was made of sterner stuff.

He took off down the path, and as his stride was much longer than Susannah's, he quickly caught up to her again, taking her arm in a firmer grip this time.

"Mr. Smollett, you are becoming a nuisance," she said.

"Miss Grainly, I don't think I have made my intentions clear to you," he said, showing some teeth. "I find you most attractive."

"Well, I don't find you attractive in the least, especially when you are standing in my way like that." She tried to push past him.

"Miss Grainly—Susannah, if I may be so bold—I assure you, you will be pleased to have my friendship when you are married to Westbridge and discover what a cold fish he really is."

"Mr. Smollett, you are becoming offensive," Susannah exclaimed. "Let me go."

"The toll is one kiss, Susannah," he said, pulling her arm so hard that it hurt her.

"Let go of me!" she cried out. She tried to kick at his shins again, but he was on to that trick by now and did not allow it. He sidestepped her easily and she caught her foot on a root and fell down. As he was still clutching her arm tightly, he came down with her.

"Now this is more like it, Susannah, my dear," he said, grabbing at her dress. The thin muslin ripped away from her shoulder as she resisted his clumsy embraces, kicking and screaming. "I like a girl with spirit, but there is no need to overdo it, my dear. You just relax, and I'll show you what it is like to be kissed by a real man, instead of that dressed-up waxwork you are engaged to."

But before he was able to give this demonstration, his attentions ceased abruptly, and Susannah was amazed to watch him move away from her as if he were levitated, until she saw the two strong arms that had effected this trick.

175

"Sandy!" she cried joyfully. "Oh, thank God you have come."

"What do you mean by this, you brute?" Sandy demanded, thrusting Smollett roughly into the bushes so that he could help Susannah up. Before he could do this, Smollett regained his balance and rushed at him, but he was no match for the Scotsman, who had been hardened by months of farm labor. Sandy hit him only once, a hard crack to the jaw, and Smollett was snuffed out like a candle.

"You haven't killed him, have you?" Susannah asked in a hushed voice.

"Nae, though he deserved it well enough," Sandy said, reaching out a hand to help her to her feet.

"Oh, Sandy, I cannot—I really have twisted my ankle this time." She gave a little laugh on the edge of hysteria.

"Now, now, don't cry, lassie. I'll get you home safe and sound." He looked over at Smollett with distaste. "I canna leave him lyin' there like that. He'll take a chill." Quickly he removed his coat and placed it over the inert form. Then, returning to Susannah, he scooped her up into his arms as if she weighed no more than a baby and proceeded to carry her to Birchwood Hall.

"Are you really Alexander Grainly?" Susannah asked him.

"There will be time enough later to speak o' that. For now, I need all my breath just to carry you. You're a healthy, strappin' girl, Susannah."

She smiled as she snuggled against his shoulder, liking the feel of his strong muscles through his shirtsleeves. "It makes no difference to me," she murmured, "but whatever will grandmamma say?"

~◎《 CHAPTER TWELVE 》◎~

LADY GRAINLY SEALED the letter she had just finished writing and glanced at the clock. It was five minutes to the hour. Lord Westbridge would be soon returning with her girls, and she wished to greet him in the drawing room, where she could offer him some refreshment. She placed the letter on a tray with two others that were ready to be posted; Trunkett would take them into the village on Monday when she went to do her errands.

She passed into the drawing room, making sure that Simons had set out glasses as ordered. There they were, sparkling on a tray, a dish of dry biscuits arranged on the table beside the decanters of sherry, brandy, and port. Lady Grainly nodded her approval. It was truly amazing how the servants had improved since Susannah's engagement. A little money made a world of difference.

The clock on the mantelpiece chimed eight. Since it had

been repaired it kept excellent time, and as Lord Westbridge was always scrupulously prompt, Lady Grainly expected him at any moment. She lowered herself into her favorite chair and arranged her skirts around her.

At five past the hour, Lady Grainly began to grow impatient. It was so unlike Lord Westbridge to be late. She polished her eyeglass with a lace handkerchief and peered at the clock once again. It was definitely five past, coming on quickly to six past. She would have a word or two to say about the matter to his lordship.

At last came the anticipated sound of the doorbell and she heard Simons answer it quickly (what a wonderful thing it was to have money again). She cocked her head expectantly toward the door, but Simons did not enter to make the announcement. She heard a brief murmur of voices, then the door burst open to reveal her granddaughter in the arms of a strange man.

"What is the meaning of this?" Lady Grainly demanded, rising with the aid of her cane.

The man came in and deposited Susannah on the settee. "Forgive my intrusion, my lady," he said politely but quickly. "Miss Grainly has had an accident. I have asked your man to send for the doctor, but he seems t' be in a wee bit o' a quandary. If you could—"

"If you please, my lady," Simons interrupted, "young Will is still at the fête, and Cook and Mary have the evening off, too."

"Where is Trunkett, then?" Lady Grainly asked, dealing with this small problem efficiently before turning her attention to the larger matter at hand. "Send for her at once."

"Yes, my lady," Simons said with relief. He would have done this himself, but in the tight hierarchy of the servants' hall he could not give orders to the lady's maid without the proper authorization.

"Have you any brandy, my lady?" Sandy asked.

Lady Grainly gestured to the table, then turned to Susannah. "What has happened? Where are Lord Westbridge and Lucy? Have they met with an accident as well?"

"I don't know where they are," Susannah said weakly. "Ivor received a note and then left me alone at the fête."

Lady Grainly frowned. "Why should he do that? What has happened?"

"She was attacked, my lady," Sandy explained, bringing the brandy to Susannah.

"Attacked?" Lady Grainly repeated, clutching her heart as she sat down again. "This is too distressing. Where is Trunkett with my smelling salts? Susannah, how could you allow yourself to be attacked?"

"I certainly did not allow it, grandmamma," Susannah said, sipping the brandy. "It was that awful Smollett, from Westham Park."

"Smollett? Do you mean that ingratiating young man with all the teeth?"

Susannah nodded.

"Not a young man to be trusted, I would have said, and it seems I was right. What was Lord Westbridge about to leave you in the care of one such as he? Oh, my poor heart! I shall have words for him if he ever shows up. Oh, Trunkett, at last. Where are my salts?"

Trunkett handed her the bottle, which was always ready for such an emergency, and cast a disinterested glance at the other two in the room. She registered no surprise, as if they presented exactly the sight she had anticipated.

"Trunkett, you must go for the doctor at once," Lady

Grainly said as soon as she was sufficiently restored. "Miss Susannah has been injured."

"Yes, my lady," Trunkett said, and without another word she left to carry out this order, passing Simons's shadow in the hallway.

"Susannah, your dress is torn!" Lady Grainly observed this fact for the first time, horrified. "You must go upstairs at once and change it before the doctor arrives!"

"I cannot, grandmamma. I have twisted my ankle."

"This is most improper, most distressing. I suppose I must fetch you one myself, you certainly cannot remain like *that*. If only I had thought of it before Trunkett left." She lifted her eyeglass briefly to examine the strange young man who was standing quietly at Susannah's side. She had no time for introductions now, but felt she was safe in leaving Susannah alone with him for a moment. Evidently, he had rescued her from the despicable Smollett and therefore could be trusted. While his accent was strange and unpleasant to her ears, it was not uneducated. The man was clearly a gentleman. One point, however, troubled her.

"Young man, have you no coat that you come to call upon us in your shirtsleeves?"

Sandy smiled slightly at the notion that she considered this visit of his a formal call. "I am afraid I had to use my coat to cover Smollett, my lady," he explained. "We left him lying on the ground and I did not want him to catch a chill."

"That was very thoughtful of you, but you really must be dressed. I will bring you one of my son's coats." She rose to her feet with an effort.

"If you would rather I went upstairs for you, my lady," Sandy suggested, noticing her affliction.

"Certainly not, although it is kind of you to offer. If I wanted to have a man rummaging through my grand-daughter's things, I could just as easily send Simons. Do help yourself to a drink while I am gone," she added graciously.

When she had left, Susannah caught Sandy's eye and giggled.

"Feelin' better, then?" he asked, helping himself to some brandy as he had been told.

"I was afraid she would ask for an introduction, and I didn't know what I would say. If I told her your real name she might have gone into a dead faint and you would have two invalids on your hands, and if I told her you were father's tenant, she would send you out to the kitchen."

"It seems t' me she must learn the truth soon enough. My masquerade has ended."

"Why, Sandy?" Susannah asked. "Why did you come here incognito?"

"It wasna my original wish. I wrote to your father, askin' if I might come for a visit. Considerin' I'm the heir, it wasna an unreasonable request t' make. He assured me, however, that my presence would mean Lady Grainly's certain death. The only way I could see the lands that would one day be mine was in the guise of a tenant farmer."

"It was very wrong of papa to suggest such an indignity," Susannah said, frowning. "I wonder that you accepted his offer."

Sandy smiled gently. "It appealed t' my sense of adventure. I had been growin' fat and stupid sittin' behind a desk and welcomed an opportunity to perform some honest toil. Then, too, I would learn about my land as few owners can, from the inside out, as it were."

"I wish I had known sooner. Why did you not tell *me*, at least?"

"I was told the very sound of my name was hateful to all the Grainlys of Birchwood Hall."

"Nonsense! You must learn not to believe everything papa says. As if anything about you could ever be hateful to me."

He regarded her seriously. "But I couldna be certain o' that—especially when I learned you were promised to another."

"I shall never marry Westbridge!" she declared, then suddenly clapped her hand to her mouth with an exclamation. "Oh, no! In all the excitement I have forgotten all about our plan. I do hope they are not at the summer house yet. Still," she added reflectively, "if they remain there all night it will turn the trick nicely."

"What are you gabbin' on about, lassie?" Sandy finished his drink and put the glass down.

"You see, I had this wonderful plan to make Westbridge marry Lucy, so I shouldn't have to," Susannah said, and briefly described her plan to him.

"You're a schemin' minx, and there's no mistake about it," Sandy said with a laugh. "And what was to happen to *you* in all this? I canna believe you did it all for your aunt's sake."

Susannah lowered her eyes shyly. "I had some idea . . . about a poor tenant farmer."

"And how do you feel about the heir to Birchwood Hall?" he asked, kneeling beside her. "Ill-educated brute that he is."

"That is not true—you went to university. I had it from Smollett himself, and you know how trustworthy he is."

"Aye, that I do," Sandy said with a sudden grimness.

"When I saw what he was doin' t' you I wanted t' break his neck."

"You very nearly did," Susannah said, absently running her fingers through his hair.

He caught her hand and pressed it to his lips. "Can you forgive me, my darlin'?"

"Forgive you for what?"

"For leavin' you alone with him like that. I didna think—I should have remembered what he was."

"I forgive you, Sandy," she said simply.

He leaned forward and kissed her.

On this tender scene burst the angry father and the wronged lover.

"What is the meaning of this?" Sir Basil demanded. Lord Westbridge, close behind him, was too stunned to say anything but fingered the pistol he had placed in his pocket, wondering if he would yet have cause to use it.

"Oh dear," Susannah squeaked.

Westbridge found his tongue at last, as the full and terrible meaning of the scene became clear to him. "Susannah, I am surprised at you! I vow I did not credit Smollett when he told us how you had gone off with this villain, who struck him down and abandoned him so mercilessly when he was trying to protect your honor."

"Pardon?" Susannah asked, confused.

"Sukey, are you all right?" Lucy asked, pushing past the two men and rushing to her niece's side. "Smollett told us what happened—all about how he tried to save you from that dreadful man."

"Did he?" Susannah asked with interest. "And about how he was trying to *protect* my honor?"

"Yes, the poor man. It was lucky his jaw was not broken. He has gone back to Westham Park with Richard to have it seen to." Suddenly she noticed Sandy for the first time and exclaimed, "Oh!"

"Look here, MacDougal!" Sir Basil blustered. "I thought I told you to keep away from my daughter." He had to strain to get the right note of indignation into his voice in the face of Sandy's implacable features.

"Do you mean this is not the first time they have been found together?" Westbridge demanded. "This is outrageous! You sirrah—" addressing Sandy "—should be locked away. Obviously, you are not a fit person for my fiancée to associate with. This is the second time tonight you have forced your unwelcome attentions upon her. Luckily, Smollett was there to stop you the first time, and we have arrived in time to stop you now."

"His attentions were not unwelcome, Ivor," Susannah said quietly.

Lucy's eyes widened, and she examined Sandy a second time with more interest.

"I see," Westbridge said coldly. "I had thought you chaste, Susannah. I see now that I was sadly mistaken."

"Now, Westbridge," Sir Basil put in, "there's no need for such language. My daughter's no wanton—it is this ruffian here who has tried to corrupt her. MacDougal, you may go now, I will speak to you in the morning."

"He shall not go!" Susannah protested. "Not until you have all learned the truth. First of all, papa, I fear you have been remiss in your manners. Lord Westbridge, may I present to you my cousin, Alexander Grainly, the heir to Birchwood Hall. Sandy, this is Lord Westbridge of Westham Park."

Sandy quite calmly held out his hand and said, "How do you do?"

Westbridge's ingrained civility overtook his confusion,

and he shook Sandy's hand before he could even think about it.

"And this is my aunt, Miss Lucy Grainly," Susannah continued. "Lucy, meet your cousin, Alexander."

Lucy turned pale and sank into a chair upon hearing the dread name for the first time. Now she managed only a weak nod and a murmured, "My pleasure, to be sure."

"I see this puts a different complexion on the matter," Westbridge said, uncertain what that complexion might be.

"And as for your precious Smollett," Susannah went on, "it was *he* who attacked me, not Sandy. Indeed, if Sandy had not been there I shudder to think what might have happened to me."

"I owe you an apology, Grainly," Westbridge said promptly and graciously.

"Thank you, my lord, but I canna accept it," Sandy answered, "because I do not deserve it. I *was* kissing Miss Grainly when you came in here, and I have kissed her before. And what is more, I shall kiss her again whenever the opportunity presents itself."

The silence that followed this statement was broken only by Sir Basil's groan.

"I see," Westbridge said at last. "Certainly, as her cousin you are entitled to show your affection from time to time."

Sir Basil breathed a sigh of relief as he saw the situation was not past remedy. "Of course, of course, they *are* cousins, after all."

Sandy smiled politely. "Beggin' your pardon, my lord, but it wasna as a cousin that I kissed her. Now, if you desire satisfaction, my lord, I would be pleased t' oblige."

"No!" Susannah and Lucy cried with one horrified voice. Westbridge ignored them and paused momentarily to consider this challenge. The issue had come down to a question of honor, and as such it was instantly comprehensible to him in all its aspects. Honor should, must, be satisfied, just as he had told Lucy earlier. And yet, he could not help but recall his recent painful experience in defending that same honor, an experience that had left him with a broken nose and wounded pride.

"I would settle for an apology, Grainly," he said at last.

"But I canna give you one, my lord," Sandy said regretfully, "for I'm na sorry for it."

They were at an impasse. Westbridge's fiancée had been defiled; he did not wish to fight a duel over it, but the other man would not offer an apology. The only thing Westbridge could do was declare his engagement to Susannah at an end. But that would be dishonorable and ungentlemanly. It was a nice point, but before Westbridge had come to any conclusions, Lady Grainly entered.

"Well, Lord Westbridge, you have finally arrived!" she said with a sniff. "You ought to be ashamed of yourself! Leaving my granddaughter in the care of that awful man who attacked her, bringing my daughter home half an hour late. It is lucky that this nice young gentleman came along when he did, or who knows what might have happened to Susannah. Here you are, Susannah. I have brought you a wrapper. I suggest you put it on at once. And here is a coat for you, young man. Now then, you have been in my house long enough. I think it is time we were introduced."

Everyone exchanged glances, no one was prepared to make the introduction.

"Does no one know this man who saved my granddaughter's honor?" Lady Grainly demanded.

Sir Basil stepped forward. "Mamma, I should like you to meet—that is, I would like to introduce—" he faltered.

"Good God, Basil, what is the matter with you? One would think it was the usurper himself, you are hesitating so."

Sir Basil and Lucy exchanged miserable glances, Susannah fussed with the strings of her wrapper. Lord Westbridge took command of the situation. He did not know why Lady Grainly should not recognize her own cousin, but he did know the right thing to do.

"Lady Grainly, may I present Alexander Grainly," he said formally.

As predicted, Lady Grainly went into a dead faint.

Fortunately, Trunkett soon arrived with the doctor, and he and Sir Basil carried Lady Grainly upstairs as she clutched her heart and moaned about the perfidy of her children. Lucy followed to render her assistance, leaving Westbridge, Sandy, and Susannah behind. Susannah might have followed, too, had her ankle not rendered her helpless.

"Would you care for a drink?" Sandy asked the other man, and Westbridge nodded. Sandy busied himself with the decanters, moving awkwardly, for Sir Basil's coat was too small for him. Noticing this, he said to Westbridge as he handed him his drink, "Is there a chance I might get my coat back? It was my best one, and there were a few wee items in the pocket that belong to Miss Grainly."

"Certainly," Westbridge replied. "I will have it sent over in the morning." He sipped his brandy. "Look here, Grainly, you seem to me to be a sensible man. Won't you reconsider about giving me that apology?"

"I'm afraid not, my lord," Sandy replied with a shake of his head.

"It makes things rather awkward, you know," Westbridge pointed out.

"Not at all. Simply break off your engagement with Susannah and all will be well."

"But I can't do that, you see." He gave Susannah an apologetic glance, as he tried to think of an alternative solution. "Perhaps if Susannah were to break it off with me?" he suggested presently.

Sandy shrugged. "One way or the other, it makes nae difference t' me. Susannah?"

Susannah nodded, a little ashamed. "Ivor, I am very sorry, but I am afraid I cannot marry you."

"Very well, Susannah, if that is what you desire," Westbridge said with dignity. "I need not mention that I am very disappointed in you." He finished his brandy and set the glass down carefully. "I will call upon your father tomorrow—there are some legal aspects to this matter he and I must discuss."

"If there is any question of monies forwarded," Sandy said, "let me know and I will inform my solicitors to cover any sum."

"Yes, that would smooth things out nicely," Westbridge said, satisfied. "I must go now. I have several little affairs to take care of at Westham Park. Smollett's dismissal, of course, and the punishment of my stepbrother for a rather nasty practical joke he played on me this evening."

Susannah gave an involuntary "oh," and Sandy looked at her gravely. "Susannah, perhaps you would care t' explain t' his lordship about your little plan. We wouldna want blame t' fall on the wrong party, now, would we?"

"Of course not, Sandy," Susannah said, then took a deep breath. "Ivor, do not punish Richard for pretending to be captured by the gypsies. It was my idea entirely."

Bravely, she took all blame onto herself, deciding the duchess was best left out of this.

"I see," Westbridge said, exhibiting no surprise nor indeed any other emotion. "May I be so bold as to inquire the reason behind such a heartless hoax?"

"It was not so very heartless, was it?" Susannah asked in a small voice. "After all, you were not kept in suspense so very long, were you?"

"It is not my own discomfort I am thinking of, Susannah, but that of your aunt. She chanced to meet me at the summer house and passed a very disturbing hour there in vigil with me."

"She didn't *chance* to meet you, Ivor," Susannah told him, avoiding his eyes.

"What do you mean?"

She hesitated. "Tell him, lassie," Sandy prompted.

"I sent Lucy there to meet you," Susannah explained with an effort. "The idea was that she should meet you there, and then we would come along and find you together, and you would have to marry Lucy instead of me."

"I see," Westbridge said frigidly. "And may I ask why such a subterfuge was necessary? Why did you not simply tell me that you did not wish to marry me? I would have released you from our engagement readily, as I did only a minute ago."

"Well," Susannah said, "I could not do that, Ivor. You see, one of us *had* to marry you—for the money." She was cold with shame. The whole thing sounded so despicable and underhanded.

"I see," Westbridge repeated. "I am surprised at you, Susannah. How could you think I would compromise your aunt so that the finding of us together would force such a conclusion? I thought you knew me better than that. I could never act in so dishonorable a manner—but obviously, that is not a difficulty for you or for Lucy. Perhaps it is as well that our engagement has been terminated—through no fault of my own." He spoke sharply, his sharpness intensified by the knowledge that he was not as blameless as he pretended to be; there had indeed been something to see at the summer house, and if he and Lucy had been discovered things would have transpired just as Susannah planned. Plainly, Lucy had learned her part well; he had fallen easily into the trap.

"Good evening," he said curtly, taking his leave before he could be humiliated further. "It was a pleasure meeting you, Grainly. Don't bother to ring. I know my own way out." But Simons was waiting in the hallway to see him out the door nonetheless.

As soon as he left, Susannah burst into tears. "Oh, Sandy, what shall I do? He was right—I am dishonorable."

"Now, now, lassie." He knelt beside her and stroked her hair in a soothing manner. "You're young and headstrong and couldna know what an effect your plan would have."

Someone cleared his throat and they looked up to see the doctor standing in the doorway. "Excuse me, I have seen to my other patient. I think it is time to have a look at you, Miss Grainly."

In a few minutes, Sandy carried her up to her bedroom, where she had her ankle examined. It turned out to be no more than a sprain, and the doctor bound it tightly and warned her to keep off her feet as much as possible.

On his way out, Sandy met Sir Basil.

"Well," the older man said in a huff, "I hope you are satisfied now. My mother is on her deathbed, thanks to you." His mouth twitched violently.

"The doctor has just told me she is resting comfortably," Sandy said.

"Only because she is drugged." He shook his head miserably. "I should have listened to her from the first and never allowed you to come to Birchwood. The blood of the Grainlys runs too thin in you—you have none of the finer sensibilities, no trace of honor, no knowledge of what it is to be a gentleman. I'll thank you if you'll leave my land in the morning and never return until I am in my grave."

"Nae, Sir Basil, I think not," Sandy said calmly.

"What's the matter with you? Can't you see that you are not wanted here? Are you not content with having ruined me and caused my mother's death as certainly as if you placed a knife in her heart?"

"That remains to be seen. As for ruining you, I think when I have married your daughter, suitable financial arrangements can be made."

"You will never marry my daughter!"

"I will," Sandy told him. "I am disappointed in you, Basil. I had thought in these last few months we had become friends. I shall return in the mornin' when you have had time t' reconsider your hasty words and perhaps repent of them."

⚖️ CHAPTER THIRTEEN ⚖️

NO ONE EVER knew how Trunkett came by her information. Certainly, she could not be in two places at once, although Susannah often suspected her of this. Just as certainly, she was out fetching the doctor the night before and could not have witnessed directly the scene in the drawing room. Perhaps it had something to do with a lengthy conference she had with Simons in the early morning, although the two retainers had never been the closest of confidants. Still, the fact remained that she was remarkably well informed on all the particulars of what took place in the drawing room last night, even during the times of her absence, and faithfully related these particulars to her mistress as soon as possible.

Lady Grainly had passed quite a restful night, aided by a few drops of laudanum from the doctor. The attack of the heart she feared she would succumb to upon actually meeting the usurper face to face was successfully averted, and she could begin to think—even calculate—about that fateful meeting. Trunkett's information gave her more food for thought, and at ten o'clock she sent for her son.

Unlike his mother, Sir Basil had passed a sleepless night worrying about Lady Grainly's health and the future of Birchwood Hall. The force of his guilt was immense. He had been the sole agent of Alexander Grainly's sojourn here. It had begun innocently enough, with his acceptance of several loans from the heir—small ones, to be sure, for he did not wish to arouse any suspicions with sudden extravagant spending. He formed a liking for the man through correspondence and soon found himself encouraging his kinsman to come to Birchwood. He had welcomed him warmly, befriended him, listened to his advice, and now the man had repaid him by stealing his daughter's affections so that even the alliance with Westham that was to be Birchwood's salvation was now impossible.

Sir Basil entered his mother's bedchamber, expecting to receive her deathbed wishes, and emerged half an hour later chastened but relieved. He immediately set out upon the errand Lady Grainly had given him, and she summoned her daughter and granddaughter to her side.

Lucy and Susannah entered tentatively, expecting, as Sir Basil had, to find her on her deathbed at the very least. The expression on her face was awful, but it was not that of a corpse.

"And how is your ankle this morning, Susannah?" she asked, the strength of her voice one that could never be supported by a weak and dying heart but only by a heart full of robust health and further bolstered by the righteous anger of its owner.

"It pains me a little, grandmamma," Susannah answered, "but it is not broken."

Lady Grainly nodded. "You had best sit down. You, too, Lucy. Both of you, draw your chairs up to the bed where I can see you—and don't fidget. A lady always sits calmly, with her hands folded in her lap if she has no needlework with which to occupy them." She sniffed at the bottle of salts she held in her hand.

They obeyed her and were both soon sitting as directed.

"First of all, I must say how disappointed I am in both of you, but most of all in you, Lucy. You are older and one would hope more responsible. How did it come about that you left Susannah alone at the fête?"

"I was not going to leave her for long, mamma—only until I fetched the shawl you left at the summer house," Lucy explained.

Lady Grainly nodded. This was the answer she had expected. Naturally, she had heard all about Susannah's thwarted plan from Trunkett, but could not believe that Lucy had been a party to it. She was now proven right by Lucy's innocent answer. "I left no shawl at the summer house," she told her daughter, "nor did I send you a note to fetch one."

"But mamma, you did!" Lucy was suddenly afraid that the recent trauma had broken her mother's mind.

"I tell you I did not," Lady Grainly said firmly, then fixed her eyes upon Susannah. She did not need to say anything more.

"I—I wrote the note, Lucy," Susannah said in a low voice.

"You wrote it? But I don't understand. Why should you want me to go to the summer house?"

"So you would meet Westbridge there," Susannah

explained, "so that we could come and find you in a compromising position and force Westbridge to marry you." She blurted this out quickly, feeling it was best to get the worst over with as soon as possible, then went on to explain in greater detail how easily Lucy had been tricked. Lady Grainly listened with interest, for there were a few points even Trunkett had been ignorant of.

"Oh!" Lucy cried when Susannah had finished, flushing red to the roots of her hair. "How could you do such a despicable thing?"

"It seemed like a good idea at the time," Susannah offered weakly.

Lucy covered her face with her hands. "Oh, I am ashamed! I am humiliated! What must Ivor think of me?"

"Stop that nonsense this instant, Lucy," Lady Grainly said severely.

"But mamma, whatever shall I do? Susannah, how could you have deceived me so?"

"I did not mean to deceive you, Aunt Lu. I thought you would be happy married to Westbridge."

"Happy? How can I even face him again? He must think that I am in on this, too, and I would not blame him if he never spoke to me again."

"Why should he think that?" Susannah asked her reasonably. "As far as he knows, you went there only to find grandmamma's shawl."

"I wish I could believe you, but I cannot."

"That is enough, both of you!" Lady Grainly took another sniff of her vinaigrette before she spoke again, with a small measure of disgust. "To think that my blood flows in both your veins! One of you is an artful little intriguer, the other a spineless nothing. You should have married Westbridge years ago, Lucy. Then we might have avoided a great deal of trouble."

"But he never offered for me, mamma. What could I have done?"

"You could have done *something*. Instead, you have sat quietly all your life waiting for things to happen to you, instead of making them happen yourself. I would not have encouraged you to go to the lengths Susannah has, but you have pursued a course of total inaction, which is quite as bad in its own way."

"I have never gone against your wishes, mamma."

"No, you have been the perfect footstool. I could not have wished for a better drudge to ease my twilight years. Be off with you—you are a nothing, a nil."

Lucy's infrequent anger was finally aroused. She straightened herself and fixed her mother with a proud glare. "You have no reason to speak to me like that, mamma, no reason to find fault with my behavior. I have always obeyed you in all things—done exactly as you wished."

"You knew I wished for you to marry Westbridge twelve years ago, yet you did nothing about it."

"This is intolerable!" she protested.

"You are intolerable! Be off with you!"

"Yes, I will be off." She rose. "I find both of you sickening. You, mamma, that you can be so ungrateful for the untiring service and obedience I have always rendered you, and you, Susannah, not because you have hurt me but because you could treat a fine, noble man like Ivor as no more than a pawn in your trivial little game."

"Well, why don't you do something about it?" Lady Grainly suggested.

"I will do something about it!" Lucy declared, fighting back tears. "Both of you talk about Ivor as if he were no more than a commodity, a resource that must be closely guarded to provide money for your wants and needs. Does neither of you realize that he is a living, breathing human being with wants and needs of his own?'' She would have said more, but she was so overcome with emotion that she could not get the words out. She gave a final inarticulate cry and rushed from the room.

Lady Grainly viewed her hasty exit complacently, then turned to Susannah. ''Now that I have taken care of Lucy, I will deal with you. I would be pleased to know if you have any further intrigue planned.''

Susannah gave her grandmother a glare just as firm as Lucy had used a minute before. ''It is no use arguing with me, grandmamma,'' she said. ''I am going to marry Alexander Grainly.''

Lady Grainly nodded quietly. ''Just as I thought. I believe that is an excellent idea. I found him to be quite a pleasant young man, although I fear I will never become accustomed to his queer accent.''

Lucy set off for Westham Park a few minutes later on foot, determined for the first time to take her fate into her own hands. She had no idea how she would begin her interview with Ivor; she only knew that she must convince him she had no part in the dastardly trick that had been played upon them. Even if she never saw him again, if he decided, quite justifiably, to have nothing more to do with the Grainlys, she could not allow him to pass out of her life believing that she would stoop to such a low trick to force him into marriage.

She had gone barely half the distance when she saw a horseman approaching, and it did not take her long to recognize the form as the one she sought.

"Ivor," she called faintly as he rode toward her, "I was just coming to call upon you."

"And I was on my way to Birchwood Hall," he said, dismounting. "I have a few legal matters to discuss with your brother, and I have your cousin's coat to return to him. I will walk with you back to the Hall."

They walked for a few yards in silence until Ivor said, "Did you have something specific to discuss with me, Miss Grainly, that you were coming to call at Westham Park?"

"Yes," she said faintly. His icy tones made her feel weak with despondence, but he offered no supporting arm. "I wish to apologize on Susannah's behalf for the trick that was played on you last night."

"On Susannah's behalf? And what of your own behalf?"

"The fault was not mine. I have no need to apologize," she said more strongly.

"No, I suppose not. You performed your part admirably. It was Susannah who let the plan fail, by not appearing at the proper moment. You must have been very disappointed, although you concealed it very well."

"Ivor, it is unlike you to speak so callously. You must believe me when I tell you that I had no idea I would find you at the summer house, no idea that Richard's supposed kidnapping was an elaborate ploy to bring you there. I would tell you to ask Susannah for confirmation if you cannot believe me, but I would rather you took my word for it. It is the word of a woman who would never knowingly deceive you."

He paused and looked down on her. "What upset me most was the thought that your bravery, the courage you showed, was nothing more than that—a mere show."

"I was not brave in the least, Ivor—I was terribly frightened."

"My dear Miss Grainly, listen to an old soldier—one shows the most courage only when one is most frightened." He spoke more gently now. "Forgive me for doubting you, Lucy. It was against all my instincts to do so, but the circumstances seemed to argue otherwise."

"There is nothing to forgive, Ivor, as long as I know you have kept your faith in me."

"You will always have that, Lucy. I will try to forget what happened last night."

They continued on their way, Lucy wondering if that was the end of it all. Last night it had seemed that they both spoke with one voice, shared one heart, but this morning there was a vast distance between them. Could nothing reach across that gap?

"I will be leaving for London tomorrow morning," Ivor remarked conversationally.

"Of course," Lucy said flatly; she had expected to hear as much but could not prevent the curious sinking of her heart.

"There is no reason for me to remain in the country," he continued. "My engagement to Susannah has been broken off." His shoulders slumped suddenly and he sagged against his horse. It was as if whatever spark of pride that supported him had suddenly departed. "Lucy, what is wrong with me?" he asked in a tight voice. "Have I some deformity I know nothing of, some fault of character that makes me disgusting?"

"Of course not, Ivor, why should you think such a thing?" she asked with some surprise.

"Because it seems as hard as I have tried there is no lady who wishes to be my bride. I have engaged myself to two ladies already, and each of them has acted in the same way—by throwing me over. I have always tried to behave honorably and convince them that my only desire was to be a good and true husband, but that was not enough, it appears. Obviously, the fault lies in myself, not in them."

"You are quite mistaken, Ivor," Lucy said quietly. Even as his spirits grew more depressed, hers surged up and gave her new hope. For the first time in her life someone needed her; someone who had always been so strong and sure was now reaching out to her for strength. Because he needed her, she found the courage to reach out her hand and take his, the courage to say, "I know where there is one who would be proud to be your wife and would prove herself as good and true as you could ever be."

He smiled slightly, a tinge of self-deprecation in his countenance. "There is no need for you to sacrifice yourself so nobly just to soothe my feelings. I must learn to live with myself as the world finds me."

"Would you not rather know yourself as I find you?" she asked. "Ivor, we may have been tricked into our meeting at the summer house last night, but no trick in the world would have sent me into your arms had I not wished to be there with all my heart. What happened between us was unplanned—and inevitable."

"Even if I believed that, how could I offer myself to you now? A broken man who has been jilted twice."

"You *must* believe it, for it is true. And you are not a broken man. It is only your pride that has been wounded a little. And Ivor"—she smiled slightly—"if I were forced to name one fault that you might suffer from perhaps it would be an excess of pride. Even now it is only pride that tells you to return to London so you will not have to face those who made a fool of you.''

He looked at her searchingly and just as searchingly into his own heart and knew she was right. It was nothing more than pride that blinded him to Lucy's love all these years, because he could not see beneath the plain and simple surface to the steadfast heart that was concealed within. Pride alone kept him so inflexibly drawn to his ideal of honor, even when wisdom told him it would not be amiss to bend now and then. Yes, he was a proud man, and it nearly choked him to swallow that pride at last, but swallow it he did.

''Even knowing this great fault of mine, Lucy, would you accept me now?''

''With all my heart, Ivor.''

He reached out to her and she came into his arms gladly. ''Then be my bride, Lucy.''

''It is the one thing I have longed for all my life,'' she told him simply.

Susannah left her grandmother's side with a lightness of heart she would have thought impossible only a few minutes before and went downstairs to the drawing room to await Sir Basil's return with Alexander Grainly.

She did not have long to wait. Sandy had accepted Sir Basil's apology eagerly and was glad to hear that he had caused no one's death, however indirectly. He was basically a simple man, not one to hold a grudge or nurse a grievance and did not argue when his cousin invited him to return to the Hall. Sandy was anxious to conclude a certain matter that had only been touched on the night before with the daughter of the house.

Sir Basil left them alone in the drawing room after only

a few minutes of idle chatter during which he received the distinct feeling that he was *de trop*.

"Ye maun forgi' me, miss, for callin' on ye in my dirties," Sandy said when they were finally alone, "but my guid Sunday kirk coat has been put t' other uses."

Susannah laughed. "No need to apologize, my good man," she said in her most nasal tones, "I have seen you in that coat many times, and I know the stains upon it come from honest labor."

"Aye, that's true enough," he agreed.

They gazed at each other in silence for a few moments, until Susannah blurted out, "Isn't it wonderful, Sandy? My grandmother approves of our marriage."

"Now, isna that a fine thing, when I havena even proposed t' ye yet."

"But I thought—last night you said—" Susannah stopped, suddenly unsure of herself. "Didn't you discuss this with papa?"

Sandy laughed. "Dinna fash yourself, lassie, I'll marry you right enough and make an honest woman o' you, as the sayin' goes. It's just that I'd like the privilege of proposin', as any man would."

She smiled. "Certainly, Sandy, I quite understand. I do hope your proposal is nicer than the others I have received."

"Others? Do you mean I've another rival besides his lordship? I'm not sure I've the courage t' issue another challenge."

"You had best not," she told him gravely, "Richard would take you up on it. But you needn't worry. I doubt that he meant his proposal seriously."

"Yet another lord toyin' with your affections! I'm afraid a proposal from me will be a comedown for you, lass. How can you listen seriously to a wine merchant and erstwhile farmer after havin' heard the earnest entreaties o' twa peers o' the realm?''

"I will try to make the adjustment," Susannah said. "Perhaps if you get on your knees it will improve things."

"Gettin' on my knees reminds me only too well o' weedin' my wee garden, but if that is what you wish, who am I t' disoblige?" He sank to his knees as she had requested. Then taking both her hands in his, he asked her in his broadest accent, "Wud ye be so kind as t' marry me, lass?"

"Of course, I will marry you," Susannah laughed. "Now, do get up."

"Is it not the custom t' seal the bargain with a kiss?"

"It certainly is," Susannah told him, and he took her in his arms. But as he embraced her, she felt a hard obstruction in his breast pocket and suddenly remembered the book of poetry that had occupied his attention so many times. She pulled away.

"What is it, lassie? You havena changed your mind again, have you?"

"No," she said quietly. "But I think if I am to be your wife I deserve an explanation of *that*," she indicated the ominous bulge, "because I could not bear to think that I was not first in your affections, that even while you were kissing me you were thinking of another, one so dear to you that you keep her memory close to your heart."

"Whatever are you goin' on aboot?" he asked, removing the book from his pocket. "I will admit I enjoyed myself while I was a farmer, but I wouldna turn t' farmin' in preference t' you."

She took the book from him and looked at the cover. It carried the quite unpoetical title *Modern Farming Techniques*.

"Oh!" she exclaimed, "I thought—"

"You thought I was pinin' for another?" he asked. He took the book from her hands and tossed it onto a nearby table. "Susannah, there has never been another besides you. Even when I thought you were nae more than a bairn, I loved you, and I shall love you until you are old and feeble."

"As I shall love you, Sandy," Susannah said, and lifted her head to meet his kiss.